SPELLBOUND

Janet McDonald

SPELLBOUND

Frances Foster Books

Farrar, Straus and Giroux • New York

Library of Congress Cataloging-in-Publication Data
McDonald, Janet, date.
    Spellbound / Janet McDonald.— 1st ed.
        p.   cm.
    Summary: Raven, a teenage mother and high school dropout living in a
housing project, decides, with the help and sometime interference of her best
friend Aisha, to study for a spelling bee which could lead to a college
preparatory program and four-year scholarship.
    ISBN 0-374-37140-7
    [1. Teenage mothers—Fiction.   2. High school dropouts—Fiction.   3. Best
friends—Fiction.   4. English language—Spelling—Fiction.   5. Afro-Americans—
Fiction.]   I. Title.

PZ7.M4784178 Sp 2001
[Fic]—dc21

                                                                00-029381

To kids,
grown and growing,
whose dreams soar on the wings of words

I thank Frances Foster for her fine editorial hand and project-girl humor, fellow author Jacqueline Woodson for her refreshing generosity, and my agent, Charlotte Sheedy, for her fierce commitment to writers. On the family tip, shout outs to the checkergirls Starlett, Natoya, Tasheesha and Makeeba, and checkerboy Kevin for keeping me close to my characters, and especially to Gwen for the artworks within.

SPELLBOUND

1

Raven flipped the baby onto his stomach for powdering and back over again for diapering before the white dust had even settled on his brown, bowed legs. It was one of the few things she felt she did really well. Being good with babies had other advantages too. Earlier that year she'd bought schoolbooks, loose-leaf paper, pens, pencils, and a knapsack to carry it all in with money she'd earned as a babysitter. She'd been so proud to put down a deposit along with the other kids on a senior class ring and graduation cap and gown. Gazing out the barred window at the distant skyline, Raven wondered if she'd be able to get her money refunded.

The clink of a key tapping on metal snatched Raven from her reverie. It wasn't hard to guess who might be paying her a visit in the middle of the afternoon on a school day. "Move your big head back from the door," she called to the eye staring into hers from the other side of the peephole, "or you'll be out there till Easter." Her mother always said even if you think you know who's out there, don't open the door until you've seen their face.

"PO-LICE! We know you in there, Raven Jefferson! Open up!"

"I know that's you, Ai, so stop clowning!" Raven said. "And you're still not getting in until I see that mug."

Aisha lived on ten, two floors down from Raven. School had made them best friends. That's usually what happens when you go to elementary, junior high, and high school together and your last names fall next to each other in alphabetical order. "Aisha Ingram, you're over here. Raven Jefferson, you're next to her." It had been that way every year from first grade to the beginning of their sophomore year. That's when Aisha dropped out.

Aisha kept on clowning. "Lady, we don't want nobody to get hurt! But we gots to take you in. You can't be walking around out here with that peasy hair!"

Raven unhooked the door chain, unlocked the bolt, and slid the steel police-lock rod out of its latch. It was stupid not to open the door when she already knew who was out there. Her mother always wanted her to do stuff that didn't make sense. "Ya mama's hair's peasy!" she snapped as Aisha bounded into the apartment. "And don't wake the baby. I just gave him his bottle."

All breasts and hips and barely five feet two, Aisha was big. She could've passed for a grown woman. Except for that baby face. Raven, a good four inches taller, was square-shouldered and lean. She liked to tease her friend about all the times

Aisha's smooth, baby-fat face stopped them from getting into clubs, even *with* fake ID. That is, way back when they used to go out.

"So what it be, Rave par-tee? Check out my braids, they phat, right? I *had* to do something. They were getting fuzzy and coming aloose. Got the nails done too! Polka dots. How ya like me now?" They sat on the vinyl-covered couch Raven's mother had recently got off layaway.

"Yeah, they're nice. Where'd you get the hair?"

"Right downtown at the Brooklyn Mall. Three packs for five dollars. Teesha, that girl on the ninth floor, did it for me. She was trying to get fifteen dollars! I was like, no, uh-uh, everybody else be charging ten, so why you gotta be like that?"

Raven was always glad to see her buddy, but especially lately. Aisha's endless gossipy stories helped Raven stop worrying. At least for a while. "So what'd she say?"

Aisha wobbled her head from side to side. "Then she gonna be like, 'Well my sister Keeba be charging twenty, so you getting a mad bargain from me.' "

"Yeah, those Washington sisters *are* money hungry. That's why I go to Toya on the first floor."

"They worse than money hungry, Rave, they money HONgry. They trying to jack up the hair prices in this building, with one sister charging plain too much and the other one charging way too much and we caught in the middle. But Holy Sister Toya ain't for me. Don't get me wrong, she my girl and everything. But I can't be sitting for all them hours with that loud church music and preaching pounding in my ears, plus with my temples steady being pulled to popping—she make her braids too tight. She's so religious but when she do your hair it's like you went to Hell instead of Heaven. I went through that one time, thank you. Did you know that before she got saved, she could driiiink? Yes, girl, we're talking Boone's Farm cheap apple wine, bottle to lips . . ."

"Lies!"

"Not! I swear on my daddy's grave."

"Aisha, your daddy's not dead. He lives in Bed-Stuy."

"Same difference. He ain't here."

"You are really ridiculous! Anyway . . . Toya's nice now and I like how she does hair. Besides, if the braids start out tight they last longer. So how much did you end up paying Teesha?"

"Only twelve. But check this out, and I got this straight outta Teesha's mouth, so it ain't gossip. Her man's in the Army, right, stationed in Germany. So guess how many times he wrote her and he been over there eight months."

"Um, let's see, a letter a day times thirty days per month, times eight months . . . two hundred forty times!" Raven chuckled to herself, knowing in advance how Aisha was going to react.

"Don't be stupid, Rave! Since when any boy gonna write a girl every day, even the ones locked up in jail with nothin' to do? These the projects, not Hollywood. He ain't sent her not one letter, postcard, smoke signal, flying bird—what they call them birds that deliver messages? . . ."

"I think I get the idea, Aisha."

". . . not a peep. And she used to do his cornrows for free. She said she glad Uncle Sam shaved that scrub's head bald as the heel on her foot. I was *dying* laughing . . . bald like her heel, she is *too* funny."

The conversation went from hair to music and back to boys. Aisha wanted so bad to go to the Puff Daddy concert but was broke as usual.

"Rap is out, romance is in," said Raven. "I would give anything for a ticket to R. Kelly's show but I got the same cash problem as you."

"What about asking your moms?"

"Please! Now *you're* the one Hollywood tripping. *That* mistake I won't make again. All she needs is the podium and the robe, because she has the sermon down pat. 'Absolutely not,' " bawled Raven in her mother's voice. " 'Don't you think you've done enough *bumping* and *grinding* already without traipsing off to hear some sex fiend sing about it? . . .' "

"At least she know the words to the song," said Aisha, laughing.

Raven continued in a singsong voice, " 'When I was growing up we listened to love songs, not sex rap . . . The Miracles, Mary Wells, the Supremes, Little Anthony . . .' I'm telling you Ai, she got me so upset I felt like I was gonna explode." She twisted a braid in her fingertips, saying nothing. "Hey, want some Kool-Aid?" She hurried to the kitchen and came back carrying in each hand a large plastic cup of bright red punch and floating ice cubes.

Aisha took a long swallow and chewed on some ice. "I don't even bother asking my moms for anything. That way, I don't have to hear her mouth."

"Our mothers want to keep living in the past, listening to old records, thinking old thoughts. R. Kelly *is* romantic. He sings about love and heartbreak and cheating and, yes, sex. Real stuff. I'm sorry but people have sex, even us teenagers."

"And got the babies to prove it," piped up Aisha before she could catch herself.

Raven shook her cup and watched the ice swirl around. "Anyway," she said slowly, like she didn't hear Aisha's comment, "maybe boys back then were singing about sweet smiles and flowers in your hair and sunshine on cloudy days and all that mess. But that was just another slick way to try to get the same thing R. Kelly's talking about. And she's one to preach, of all people."

"Right! Where they get off preaching to us when we *all* illegitimate? If they was so pure and holy, how they get us?!" Aisha bit down on a big ice cube.

"Adoption," Raven said with a shrug.

Kool-Aid splashed out of Aisha's mouth, then she started coughing and laughing and coughing some more. Pointing to her throat, she got out, "Ice, ice."

Laughing, Raven slapped her on the back. "I told you about eating ice! Now look at Mommy's couch! Thank God for that plastic cover!"

"It's your fault. You made me laugh! And stop hitting my back, you do it too hard! You gonna kill me saving me."

They wiped the couch with paper towels, still giggling. This was the kind of moment Raven loved, hanging out, feeling lighter, less burdened. Wearing knee-length overalls, she lay back on the couch and stretched her long legs across Aisha.

Aisha was looking at Raven's scarred knees when she asked, "So, how it feel?"

"How does *what* feel? You know I've had these scars since I was a ten-year-old wild tomboy."

"Not that. I mean motherhood."

Raven hesitated. "I really don't know, Ai. Like I'm babysitting somebody else's baby."

2

isha saw on Raven's face the same look she'd seen in the mirror after having her own baby two and a half years ago. She wanted to say that this was the hardest part, that things would get better, but instead she just tried to make Raven laugh. "Well, if you ask me, Smokey *is* somebody else's baby. Just look at them green, see-through, demon eyes."

"Hazel, Aisha, they're hazel."

"Wha-ever. They still see-through." Aisha picked up a framed color photograph of a red-faced bundle dressed in a blue jumper and tiny blue high-top sneakers. "You remember that old movie we saw, the one with what's her name, you know, her husband's that short guy with the glasses who took naked pictures of their daughter? . . . Boy, if my man did that to my kid, I would bust him up . . ."

Raven tapped her foot and hummed to drown out Aisha. What was she talking about? That girl could never get out one simple story without going all around the block and up and down ten side streets.

Aisha snapped her fingers. "I got it! Farrell. No, Farrow. Maya Farrow!"

Raven squinched up her face. "You mean *Rosemary's Baby*?"

Aisha frowned in the direction of Smokey's photo. "You said it, not me."

"Skank!" Raven grabbed a handful of Aisha's brand-new store-bought braids. "I'll give you Rosemary's Baby . . . Say you're sorry! Say it or I'll snatch these off and sell them!"

Aisha tried to say "sorry" but was breathless from laughing. All she could get out was "Ah-ight! Ah-ight!" She clutched her scalp, where the new hair was sewn into the old.

"That does not sound like a 'sorry' to me, Rosemary." Raven tugged.

"Ah-sah! Sah! Sorry!"

Raven released the shiny black locks. "All right, that's better. And by the way, you and little Starlett are straight outta *The Omen*, Parts One *and* Two."

Raven could hardly believe that Smokey was three months and twelve days old. When her mother found out Raven was having a boy she came up with the name Smokey, after one of those old-school singers she was always listening to on the classic soul radio station. Raven didn't want the baby to be named after some golden oldie but how could she refuse her mother after letting her down the way she had? The newborn's hazel eyes and light skin made it seem like maybe he'd been given the right name after all. He *did* look like that singer Smokey Robinson. "Rave honey, don't he look about ready to jump up and start singing 'Mickey's Monkey'?" her mother had joked at the hospital. Raven was sure that getting to name the baby was why she had stopped being mad and started acting proud to be a grandmother.

Raven shook a finger in Aisha's face. "If you woke up my baby with your loud self," she said, "you're in trouble."

Aisha waved her off. "Girl, let me tell you something about these project babies. They sleep through anything, loud music, police sirens, fire truck horns . . . the ones in the City probably slept right through that Twin Towers bomb. Remember all the shooting that was going on around here when I was pregnant with Starlett . . . two, three o'clock in the morning—bang! bang!—like they was cowboys? Teesha said these dudes from Albany projects was looking for Mookey Williams over some girl he . . ."

"Get to the point, Poindexter."

"If you let me fin . . . ish what I'm trying to say, *thank* you . . . What I'm trying to say is . . . now you made me forget . . . oh, yeah, these babies, they can sleep, let me tell you."

"That's *it*? I thought you were saying something about when you were carrying Starlett."

"Well, now I really did forget 'cause of your big mouth." Aisha shifted her hips on the couch. "This plastic make my butt sweat and it ain't even summer. Look how my butt's sweating. Can't y'all get cloth?"

12

"At least we *have* a couch."

"Wha-ever."

Sometimes Raven wanted to take Aisha by the shoulders and shake her until all the loose pieces in her brain fell into place. But Ai was her girl. When Raven found out about being pregnant, she was too afraid to tell her mother right away. It was the first time she'd ever fooled around with a boy, trying to act all grown at that stupid make-out party the Washingtons had given while their mother was in Atlantic City. She didn't even know him but everyone else was kissing and rubbing up on each other and everything. And to go with him in that dark room . . . Then she lost hold of her world. First, he didn't phone her like he said he would. But what boy ever does keep a promise to call? Then her period didn't come. That was scary. And didn't come. And didn't come. God, if only she could go back in time and do things differently. All she knew about him was his first name. She kept going to school and paid down on the ring and graduation stuff like the rest of her class, except the ones who knew they weren't getting promoted. She dodged questions about her weight and prayed the problem would go away by itself.

When it didn't, she turned to Aisha. Crazy as Aisha was, she could be serious when she had to, and pretty sensible. "You're a trimester too late to even think about anything but having it. Damn, I hate to see you ending up like me. I wasn't going nowhere nohow with my bad grades, but you . . . you supposed to be going to college. Well, like my mama say, all that's ancient

13

history now. We gotta deal with the real now, Rave. First thing, you gots to tell your moms. 'Cause she *will* find out. And go to that baby clinic. I can hook you up with the same nurse I had. She be getting in your business but she cool. And you don't need the mad stress of school at a time like this—I would say chill on that until all this is over." Yeah, Ai had helped her a lot. But Raven hoped Aisha was wrong about one thing—that her shot at college was now ancient history.

Aisha suddenly shook her head as if just waking up. "I remember! I'd feel Star kicking in me each time a gunshot went off. But once she came out, noise didn't bug her one bit. Like she got used to the world before she was even in it."

Raven wished she could get used to her new world too. "Then I need to take some lessons from Star because I'm still trying to get my bearings, what with no sleep, smelly diapers, and baby spit-up. But the worst part is being cooped up all day with a baby, bored. When it's somebody else's and you're just waiting for them to come home and pay you, that's different, but when it's you with your own . . . You know, Ai, if you don't come by I mostly sit here with nobody to talk to, watching people throw chairs on talk shows. I have nothing to do and a million things to do at the same time. Nothing to do for me, a million things to do for the baby. I can't even read a book because I have to watch *him* every second."

"I hear that. I think I was out dancing once this whole year. And forget hanging out at Coney Island beach like *in the days*, not with my stretch-marked belly. It's a trip, this twenty-four/seven motherhood thing. I even miss school, and you know how much I hated it when I was there. But at least it gave you something to do, people to hang out with, a change of scene. I remember there was this girl in my gym class whose butt jutted out so far, it was like you could deliver food on it. We called her Pizza Delivery Butt . . ."

"Shhhh!" Raven thought she heard a noise. She sat still, looking toward the room she shared with the baby. It wasn't Smokey. Just the people next door making noise.

"For real, though, Rave, don't let it get you down. Lots of girls have babies, mostly by accident. Yeah, it woulda been better, easier, if we were more grown-up, with husbands and jobs and all that, but babies land when they land. You gotta deal with it, that's all. And when Starlett and Smokey are teenagers we can all party together 'cause their mothers will still be young foxes."

"Get over it, Aisha. We'll be played-out old bags listening to classic rap and our kids will be like, 'Where're *you two* going? Not with us.' " Raven looked out the living-room window. The view opened out onto the Brooklyn Bridge, a sight that always held her eyes. From a distance, the cables looked like lace held in place by massive stone arches. Plump clouds tumbled freely along. Summer was three months away and the sky spread blue as far off as she could see.

"When the housing people put in your window guards?" asked Aisha. Starlett was steady climbing all over everything and Ai was glad hers were up.

Raven's eyes, still holding sky and cloud, looked toward Aisha. "What? Um, I don't know. I think they talked to

15

Mommy." She seemed far away. Aisha asked if she was all right.

"I'm fine. Just daydreaming."

"Daydreaming? You better be dreaming about getting your little hazel-eyed devil to the exorcist." Aisha cupped her hand over her mouth to smother the laugh that roared out anyway.

Raven gripped her wrist. "All right, that's it. Up. Get out of my house before Mommy gets home. I'm not supposed to have company anyway. Up!" She pulled vigorously on her arm but couldn't budge her stout friend. All that moved were Aisha's round shoulders, trembling with laughter.

3

R aven was sitting at the kitchen table watching TV and bottle-feeding the baby when her mother walked in balancing grocery bags, a large purse, and the day's mail in her arms. It was March and the wind had blown her hair all to one side.

"Hi, Mommy. Your hair's lopsided."

"Come and help me with these bags and don't worry about my hair. Your check and food stamps came." Mommy. Raven's mother pondered the word. That was baby talk, coming from her baby who was sitting there cradling her *own* baby. She still couldn't get over it. Raven—a mother. Not even through high school yet. "And how was your day?" She leaned over and kissed Raven's forehead and Smokey's fat cheek.

"Like this," said Raven, her eyes on the television.

Her mother was used to that answer. It meant Raven was down in the dumps. "No visitors, I hope."

"I know the rules." *That* answer meant Raven had had some

friend over, probably Aisha. Otherwise, she would've said, "Nope," as usual.

Her mother took off her heavy black shoes, gray postal clerk slacks, and matching shirt in the back bedroom and returned wearing a sweatshirt and sweatpants. She stretched out on the couch. "I'm going to rest my eyes. Warm up that spaghetti from last night and when I get up I'll make some garlic bread."

Raven grunted in response without moving—the baby was dozing, its lips still gripping the bottle's milky nipple. Raven ventured a look at her mother. Lying there in sweats, long-legged and slim, she could've been Raven's slightly older sister. She looks all right for her age, Raven thought, but I wouldn't party with her.

Gwen had given birth to her first child when she was only fifteen. Her father had come close to putting her out on the street, and probably would have if her mother and the pastor hadn't joined forces and convinced him that his daughter's pregnancy was God's will. The baby's father was just sixteen, young enough to be left unfazed by the news. He kept on living his child life, undisturbed by the child he'd left her with—Dell, now twenty. And he kept hanging around, promising this and that, marriage, their own apartment, money . . . they'd have all that as soon as he got a little older.

Of course, Gwen knew better but she hadn't been able to make herself stay away from that lying boy. "In love," that's what she called stupidity back then. Three years later she was pregnant by him again. This time her father did put her out. And no amount of "Jesus talk," as he put it, was about to change his mind. She expected Bobby's family—that was the boy's name—to take her in but they wanted nothing to do with her. "Honey, that boy of mine got enough kids to start his own orphanage," huffed his mother. "If all you girls and babies start moving in here, where *we* s'pose to live?"

Luck got her a place in the projects. But that was where anything else even resembling luck came to an end. A teenage mother with two mouths to feed and no schooling wasn't exactly what you'd call blessed. Bobby moved on to other girls, she'd heard, and ended up somewhere down South. Getting on welfare was about all she could do. And study like the devil for the high school equivalency exam. Once she got that diploma, her luck came back. On her second try, she passed the post office test and they called her in for an interview. Leaving the girls with babysitters wasn't her idea of raising them up the right way but she had to work.

She'd done all a mother could do, even discussing birth control first with Dell, then with Raven. Each one had responded with blushes and squirming denials. And then Raven had come to her one night, crying. Gwen had noticed the weight change and Raven's moodiness but she had failed, or maybe refused, to put one and one together. Didn't want to see what was right there in front of her face. Raven was four months pregnant. And there was no turning back. She was "showing" and couldn't bear to go to school anymore. "I just don't want to go," she'd sobbed, "everyone's all in my business. I'm tired of sneak-

19

ing in and out the side door to avoid their looks. Please!" The child was too upset for it to make any difference to her that half her friends had babies. Like that going-nowhere Aisha, who'd dropped out of school even *before* she got pregnant. Gwen had prayed that bookish as Raven was, she'd get her diploma, maybe go to college like Dell. One thing was certain—even if her disappointment in Raven showed from time to time, she would never outright reject *her* flesh and blood because the girl made a mistake. They were still a family.

Raven watched her mother's eyelids twitch and listened to her snore. The sound startled the baby, then his body relaxed again, limp and heavy. Maybe I'll get that job they had in the paper today. Then I can help out more, Mommy won't have to work so much overtime. She considered the bundle on her lap, its warmth and weight, and listened to the hiss of air as the baby sucked from an empty bottle. He was growing real fast. Three months old and soon it would be April, then he'd be four months, May, five months . . . and on and on, for years and years. What did the future hold for them? She was scared. Please, God, please, God, please, God, if you're up there, please give me that job.

4

How could Aisha be late on such a big day? Raven tugged at her skirt for the hundredth time. The snug fit was an uncomfortable reminder of the weight she'd put on when she was pregnant. She'd lost most of it but still felt hurt when Dell said, raising one eyebrow in that superior way she had, "Employers can tell a project girl from a mile away by those truck-wide, ghetto hips and, believe you me, nobody wants to hire *that*. To succeed in this world, you have to have a downsized business body, not a teen-mom project booty." Today, Raven was aiming for success and she was about as downsized as she was going to get.

The baby was in his crib kicking and spitting. Raven pushed the pacifier in his mouth and checked her watch. Eight thirty-five. She had to be in Manhattan by nine for the job interview. The woman who'd answered the phone about the ad had said, "Nine a.m. and that means on the dot." Eight thirty-seven.

There was a commotion at the door. "Raven, I'm here! Sorry!" Raven yanked it open. Aisha was balancing Starlett on one hip and an overloaded baby bag on the other.

"You *are* sorry, Aisha, and I'm running late. You were supposed to be here at eight! The baby's in the crib. His bottles are in the refrigerator. See you around lunchtime. His diaper should be clean."

"*Should* be?" said Aisha, frowning.

"Just check it and stop complaining. I should dock your behind for being late. You have an extra token?"

"Hell, no. What you think I am, the babysitter *and* the welfare?"

Raven shot Aisha a dirty look. She could not take the chance of getting stuck in the elevator, not today, so she ran down the stairs, taking two steps at a time.

The pedestrian walkway of the Brooklyn Bridge was busy. Yuppies from the brownstones and high-rises of Brooklyn Heights. Joggers in tights with grim, determined looks on their faces. Tourists pointing cameras at this and that famous building. And Raven, excitedly hurrying toward her first job interview.

Far below, the East River churned, whipped by the wind. The rhythm of her movement was relaxing. Her feet, her legs, her thighs, all of her rising and falling, rising and falling. Even the drone of traffic speeding in both directions seemed somehow soothing. Raven was feeling her body for the first time in a long while. Instead of sitting up with the baby or lying down with the baby, her body was breathing, striding, alive. Off to her right, other bridges whose names she didn't know connected Manhattan Island to the outer boroughs. But everyone knew that the only borough that counted, the one where you might glimpse stars like Brandy and Jennifer Lopez or watch a movie being made, was Manhattan—"the City." The others were places where plain people lived, people who weren't special, people like her. She might move to the City after she'd saved up enough money from this job. Why not? She smiled at the thought.

On her left, she could see the Statue of Liberty, a symbol she'd learned about in school but had never visited. Maybe she would one day, with Smokey. A gusty wind flapped the giant American flag at the top of the bridge. It was pretty, the white stars and the red and blue against the pale sky. By the time she was gliding down the path on the Manhattan side, Raven was cheerfully planning how she'd spend her first paycheck.

5

The big hand on the wall clock had almost reached the twelve when Raven entered the offices of the National Life Insurance Company. Whew, she'd just made it—nine on the dot. She smiled at the receptionist and asked for an application. The company had advertised for a file clerk and Raven knew she was perfect for the job, if only because she needed it so badly. Other applicants were busy scribbling away on clipboards balanced on their knees.

Raven had never before filled out a job application but thought she'd figured out what it took. She concentrated on two things: her penmanship, which was extremely neat, and telling the truth. From when she was little, her mother had always said that only good could come from the truth. In the space next to "Strengths" she wrote "personality & arithmetic." For "Weaknesses" she put down "spelling." In junior high, her English teacher had said "how odd" it was that someone who read so much could be such a poor speller. Under "Special

Needs" she wrote "day care." She cringed as she checked the "No" box next to "High School Diploma," but on the whole felt good about the form she was about to hand in.

A tall boy wearing high-water pants stepped up to the desk and put his application on the stack. The receptionist glanced at it. "Someone will be in touch with you within the week. Thank you for your interest in National and have a nice day." Three girls with puffed-up hair like cotton candy handed theirs in together. Again, the receptionist said, "Someone will be in touch with you within the week. Thank you for your interest in National and have a nice day." Raven was surprised to hear her make the same speech over and over. What an easy job. She wouldn't have any trouble doing that kind of work. She gave her form one last look-over, waited her turn, and handed it directly to the woman. She waited for The Speech.

"I'm sorry, miss, every applicant must hold a high school diploma. We won't be able to process your application further. Thank you for your interest in National and have a nice day."

Raven felt the blood rush from her legs. "But . . . the ad didn't say you needed . . ."

"Miss, I'm sorry. It goes without saying that you need a diploma to get a job, any job. And we *certainly* don't provide day care."

Raven knew better than to say what she said next, but the words popped out. "A diploma's only a piece of paper. I know I would be a good file clerk."

The receptionist gave Raven a cold look. "Thank you for your interest in National and have a nice day." Then she turned away to answer the phone. "National Life Insurance, how may I direct your call?" Raven stood there, trying to think of something she could say to make this mean woman give her the job. "Is there something more, Miss . . . um"—she glanced at the top of Raven's application—"Jefferson?" Raven rushed from the office.

The walk back across the bridge was hot and suffocating. Raven's eyes teared. She told herself it was from pollution. She heard Dell saying, *Employers can tell a project girl from a mile away. Ghetto hips.* Her head buzzed with thoughts. I may not have my diploma but at least I don't have ghetto hips. But I *do* have a baby. The receptionist's words came back to her. *And we* certainly *don't provide day care.* She was stuck. A dropout. A teenage mother. A jobless project girl on welfare. Nobody wants to hire *that.*

Up ahead, two girls in tight black leggings were jumping around being loud and smacking each other on the neck. Raven recognized them from the back. It was Teesha and Keeba, the hair-braiding Washington sisters. Spinning to duck a neck slap, Teesha spotted Raven. "Rave, wassup, girl?! What you doin' up here on the stroll, working hard for the money? Hey, when you gonna let me do your hair? Look like you could use a touch-up."

Keeba asked after Smokey. "He so *fine*, Lord hold me back. When he get older, hmmm, I'm gon' be all on that."

Teesha glared at her sister. "You so stupid with your baked potato brain! He won't want your dried-up, played-out, crusty behind." Then she landed a good one on Keeba's neck and ran screaming down the walkway. Keeba gave chase.

Their huge behinds quaking like pudding made Raven laugh out loud. She *liked* ghetto hips. Her homegirls had them. Anyway, what did being a good worker have to do with hip size? Or a stupid piece of paper, for that matter.

6

aven unlocked her door but couldn't get in the apartment. "Aisha! The chain's on, come open the door! Ai!" After a good amount of clanking and rattling rang out, the chain dropped loose. The door creaked open by itself. Raven slammed it shut behind her.

Aisha half smiled. "Hey, Rave, how'd it go?"

Raven's eyes traveled down, then up the towel pulled tight around Aisha. Her bad mood got worse at the sight of Aisha standing there half naked and guilty-looking. "What's with the chain being on? I was out there banging for fifteen minutes."

"That wasn't no fifteen minutes. Anyway, I was in the shower. Wasn't no psychos breakin' in here like in that movie where the lady was showering all carefree then that big butcher knife slashed through the curtain right when she . . ."

She was in no mood to listen to Ai's nonsense. "Smokey okay?"

"Yeah, he still sleep." Aisha didn't like the look on Raven's face. "What happened to *you*, they cut off your food stamps?"

Raven sat on a chair at the table. "They said you have to have a high school diploma."

Aisha felt relieved. At least Raven wasn't mad at *her*—not yet anyway. "That ain't right. I know plenty people who got jobs without no diploma. If they want you, they hire you. Look at Tim, he been at White Castle for . . . it have to be at least two years now . . . I remember 'cause me and Patrice had gone there to eat . . . I love them square flat hamburgers. I used to eat ten at a time, I kid you not . . . but they little, so it's not like eating ten normal . . ." Aisha's rambling got worse when she was nervous.

"Aisha, *please*, you're giving me a headache. White Castle's not an office job. I'm trying to be something important, not somebody's hamburger helper."

Aisha rolled her eyes. Hamburger helper? Here she is coming back home with no job at all and she gonna be all uppity about Tim's gig. "Look, I know you want to help out your moms and all but now that you got Smokey, the system *have* to take care of y'all, no matter what. So you might as well chill, like me."

Dell was right. Aisha *did* have that "recipient mentality." Raven hit at a fly but missed. "But I don't want to be like *you*."

Aisha did not appreciate the tone of that *you*. Raven could be so *drama* at times.

"I don't want to *chill*. If Mommy had chilled she wouldn't be where she is today. I want a job. College. *Something.* Anyway, nowadays they kick you off welfare after five years, *no matter what.* So you won't be *chillin'* for long."

Aisha was hurt. "I ain't worried. My man'll be taking care of me by the time that happens." Aisha did worry sometimes about the future, how long the checks would last, what kind of workfare hell she might be forced into to keep her benefits. She didn't want to end up washing graffiti off subway walls. Her moms had warned her a long time ago that she and Starlett would be on their own if they lost their benefits.

Out of spite, Aisha said, "Anyway, you can't go to college if you ain't even finished high school. If you wasn't so choosy, Miss Office Girl, you'd *have* a gig."

A door squeaked. Footsteps approached. A boy appeared. His low-hanging jeans and oversized designer sweatshirt were rumpled. Starlett, fast asleep, was in his arms. "What up?"

Raven bristled. "What you mean, 'what up'? What are *you* doing in my house?"

Aisha cringed into her towel. "Oh, don't be like that, Rave."

"Don't ... be ... like ... *what*? You know Mommy would kill me if she found out I had some thug in here while she was at work. She said 'no company' and you *know* that, Aisha! *You're* not even supposed to be here unless it's to watch the baby."

Aisha had just about had enough of Raven's mouth, taking stuff out on everybody else just 'cause she didn't get that corny job. "Thug? Why you gotta go *there*? That's the baby's father. Kevin."

Raven looked the boy up and down. "Excuuuuse me. You mean, the father who hasn't been around in six months?"

"Oh, like Smokey's daddy been seen at all," mumbled Aisha.

Ignoring all of it, the boy said, "I'll take Star downstairs. Later."

Raven fixed her eyes on Aisha's.

"Don't be lookin' at me that way. We wasn't doin' nothin, not that it's your business. He just now got here, probably ten minutes before you knocked . . ."

"I'm so pissed at you, Ai! Don't we have enough of that kind of trouble as it is, without . . ." Raven squeezed two fingers into her skirt pocket. "Here, take your money. Thanks for watching Smokey—that is, if you *did* watch him." She strode down the hall.

Aisha disappeared into the bathroom.

7

The churchgoers plumped down on the worn wooden bench, still a little out of breath. The afternoon service had been lengthy and raucous and the women chatted with pride about the "mighty noise" the Holy Spirit had raised inside their run-down church. Veterans of the projects, they were longtimers who could rattle off the family history of anybody who walked by. They had lived in their apartments for twenty, thirty, forty years. So long that they'd forgotten they were renters who could be put out at a moment's notice. After that many years, they thought of themselves as homeowners. Magazine pictures of Martin Luther King, Jr., and the Kennedys hung on their walls in plastic frames. These old women were survivors.

A compact two-door black convertible pulled up to the curb and came to a rubber-screeching stop. The driver, a young woman, stepped out and pointed something at the car that caused it to let out a short, muffled wail. She waved at the women on the bench. Her thin frame gave her that angular, underfed look popular among white women in the City but cause for alarm in the projects. Too often slim was a warning that a person was on their way down, on drugs or real sick. Here, fat was *in*. All that flesh meant you were healthy.

But the woman approaching the group was definitely not on her way down. Her hair was permed and styled into a smooth, black French roll, and her tailored burgundy pantsuit looked soft and expensive.

Mrs. Hendricks was first to recognize the visitor. "Well, I'll be . . . the other Jefferson girl. Haven't seen that child in God knows how long. I know you're gonna give your old god-mother a kiss."

Old women often appointed themselves godmother to a neighborhood child, whether the kid wanted her or not. It was one of the few things Dell still loved about the projects. She leaned forward to kiss the gray-haired woman she'd known ever since she could remember knowing anyone. "How you doing, Ma? You look younger every time I see you."

Mrs. Simpson tugged at Dell's arm. "I know you giving me some sugar, skinny Minny." Dell winced at the name she'd grown up hating and leaned over the smiling woman nick-named Sugar because of the kisses she always wanted.

"You know I wouldn't forget my Sugar." She planted a loud kiss on her other godmother's face. "Or Miss Johnson," she added, turning to her mother's more reserved neighbor, who was shyly awaiting her turn.

"Look at you, looking like a store-window statue! And still

got them jet-black eyes," exclaimed Mrs. Johnson, holding on as Dell gently pulled away.

"I sure hope so. I wouldn't be much good without them, now would I? Okay, ladies, I have to get upstairs for Sunday dinner or they'll eat it all. You know how our people get when food's around."

The godmothers doubled over, tickled, losing their wind. They recovered long enough to tell Dell to bring them down some plates of food.

She ran into the building toward the open elevator. "Hold it!" No one inside moved as the door shut. It left without her.

Dell couldn't decide what she dreaded more—waiting for the elevator or riding in it. Waiting meant standing in the lobby. It had changed so from when she was growing up. These days trash and graffiti welcomed you inside. No matter how often the front-door window was repaired, one pane was always broken. What bothered her most, though, were the handshakes that lingered the few extra seconds it took for money and foil-wrapped crack to switch places. Then there was the ride. Moving or stopping wasn't the problem. You simply didn't know if the door would open onto your floor or into a brick wall. Dell was sure that being stuck so often between floors was what had made her claustrophobic.

The elevator bumped to a stop and Dell watched folks get off. More people poured out than that small metal box should hold. She waited again while a new load piled on, then she squeezed in. It bounced upward, its old cables creaking under the strain. A honey-colored pit bull puppy took a seat on Dell's foot. Its owner, dressed in full gangsta wear, lifted it up to his face and rubbed its nose with his own.

" 'Scuse him, he only six weeks old. Right, Homey, you just a newborn?" The sight of this tough-looking kid cooing and Eskimo-kissing a puppy made Dell smile.

"No problem. He's a cute little guy."

A young mother scolded three fidgety kids in Spanish. Dell guessed she was around Raven's age. A lanky boy in a Michael Jordan tank top held a basketball against the wall with his head. Sweat dribbled down his neck. A baby shrieked. Dell held her breath against the smell. Urine, sweat, dog, and baby. When the elevator finally reached her floor she lunged, gasping, from its hold.

In the Jefferson kitchen, all available stove space was covered. Cooking had begun early in the morning. Macaroni and cheese, collard greens, sweet potatoes, corn bread, baked chicken, spare ribs, and apple pie were steaming. Dell inhaled deeply, then exhaled, "Fooood!"

Raven felt sulky. They used to eat Sunday dinner in the evening, at dinnertime like you were supposed to. Then all of a sudden it got moved to afternoon dinner. Everything was always being changed around to suit Dell. Dinner at lunchtime—who ever heard of that? But that's what worked out best for Dell, Mommy said. She wouldn't have to drive back home too late and could get a good night's rest before work. Dell. The good daughter. College graduate and car owner. Big salary and little hips. Perfect, childless Dell. Well,

Raven sure wasn't going to help cook for the family princess. So Mrs. Jefferson had prepared the whole meal herself.

"Hey, Sis, how's tricks? How's the kid?" Dell asked, not waiting for an answer as she vanished into the bathroom.

She had promised herself on the drive over not to say anything critical about the weight Raven had put on, or the baby, or school. She loved her sister, which was why she had to push her. Raven was too bright to let her life career off course. Okay, so she got stuck with a brat like most of her friends. Still, she had to try to get back in school and on track. She had potential, and Dell had a plan.

Raven sometimes wished Dell would come by more often. She did know a lot about jobs and school and how everything worked as far as getting ahead. But most of the time she was grateful her sister lived all the way in Queens because Dell could be a pain sometimes. A lot of times, really. Dell reappeared, freshly lipsticked.

"Mommy made you a pie." One sure way to lure Dell from her apartment was with the promise of apple pie. Raven's favorite was sweet potato but they rarely had that.

"She did? Lemme at it!"

Raven smirked. "April Fool!"

"That was cold and craven. But guess what, you're a tad too late. April Fools' Day was last week. And besides, I smell my pie."

Dell dashed to the kitchen, snatched the checkered cloth napkin off the pie plate, and raised a sharp knife over the golden brown crust. Gwen lurched up from her resting position on the couch. "Dell, you better get away from that pie! Raven, did you send her running in there like a wild animal? You know you have to eat dinner first." The sisters exchanged amused looks. They did the same thing every time there was a pie, just to watch their mother's reaction.

Dell leaned down and gave her mother a kiss. "Now don't be going postal on us, Mommy dearest, we were only looking at your precious pie."

A year ago Dell had moved to her own place, right after graduating from Jay Street Community College. Couldn't wait to get out of the neighborhood. Gwen still missed having her around.

"Come and sit down beside me," she said, patting the space next to her. The thick plastic cover squeaked as Dell plopped down. "Be careful before you bust it, Dell!"

Dell was preoccupied with her idea for Raven's future but decided to wait until they were eating. Great food and easy-going conversation would smooth the way.

"Mother, I need to talk to you about something. It's kind of serious."

Gwen braced herself. Now what? Health problems? Trouble at work? Please, Jesus, not another fatherless baby.

"I'm not sure exactly how to put it . . ."

"Spit it out, Dell, you know I got pressure."

Gwen had convinced herself she had high blood pressure, despite her normal test results. It was comforting to have a physical explanation for her fears and anger and worry. No need to look any further.

"Okay, okay. Mother . . . plastic couch covers are tacky."

Gwen shook her finger at Dell and warned her about playing with sick people's pressure. The only thing between stains, marks, spots, and her nice sofa was that plastic cover and it was staying, tacky or not. The stitching on the seam already had a reddish-looking spot, like something got spilled on it. She was so proud Dell had graduated college and become a professional, even if she *was* the silliest-acting twenty-year-old God ever breathed life into.

8

Smokey sat propped up by pillows in his high chair and the women were in their usual places, Gwen at the head of the table and Raven and Dell opposite one another. "So how's paralegal life treating my child?"

"Legal assistant, thank you. It's all good in the hood. The work's kind of boring and lawyers are so obnoxious but my office mate is fun. She really is too much, that Leah. Her heavy-duty Brooklyn accent cracks me up. And she's such a basket case, always crying and claiming she doesn't know why. Then she'll say, 'Sing that sad song for me again, Dell. The Willie Nelson one, "You Were Always on My Mind." ' So I go in my low cowboy voice, *Maybe I-I-I never told you . . . I'm so hap-py . . . that'cher mine . . .* and she starts sniffling. Then she goes, 'Why am I so neurotic?' I swear, Mother, it's like sharing an office with that director, you know, that fast-talking nervous guy who did *Manhattan*."

"Woody Allen," said Raven, balancing a mound of macaroni on her fork. Why was *he* on everybody's mind?

"How do *you* know about Woody Allen? I thought you only saw movies starring rappers."

"Ha. Ha," said Raven, "I'm not *totally* illiterate."

Gwen rolled her eyes. "Don't even mention that man's name in this house," she said, pouring molasses on a thick square of corn bread. "The man done married his own daughter. Make me sick to my stomach."

"Oh, don't be so old-fashioned. She wasn't his biological daughter. He never even adopted her. They just fell in love."

"Dell, please! How's she gonna fall in love with something looking like that? The man was living there, raising that child like a father, and took advantage of the situation. Anyway, it's not what *he* thought he was, it's what that child thought he was. To her, he was 'Daddy.' "

Dell leapt at the flaw in her mother's argument. "See! See! You're wrong, because he didn't live with them. He had his own apartment. So you're jumping to conclusions like everybody else."

Raven sucked her teeth, glad to have the chance to come to her mother's defense. "Check out Miss Fake Lawyer. Your obnoxious bosses are rubbing off on you. It doesn't matter if he wasn't the real father or didn't live with them or hadn't adopted her or whatever, he's still too old for her. He's like sixty-something and she's only twenty. Aisha said she would bust him up if she was the mother. And so would I."

The sisters stared at each other. Quickly, Gwen asked for

some ice from the freezer. Her fruit punch was getting warm. Maybe if one of them got up and moved around, tempers wouldn't flare up. Nobody budged.

"Really, is that what the Girl in the Hood said?" asked Dell, raising an eyebrow. "Yeah, she *would* bust somebody up for being in love. I'm sorry, but your buddy Aisha is so project she makes the girls locked up at Rikers Island look like debutantes. Why do you hang out with that roughneck dropout?"

"Just because everybody didn't finish school like you did doesn't mean they're . . ."

Gwen shot a warning glance at Dell, who forged right ahead.

"Speaking of school," began Dell, leaning back in her seat the way she did when she was on her high school debating team, "you should've stayed . . ."

"Mommy, she's starting . . ."

"Dell, eat your food. And don't be picking on your sister. Show me one person who can claim they haven't made a mistake in this life and I'll show you . . ."

"I know, I know, somebody who would lie to their own mother on her deathbed. I'm not picking on her. It's just that if she hadn't gotten pregnant by some *homey* and quit school like all her chubby welfare-mama homegirls . . . Where *is* the father, by the way, when's *that* state secret coming out, or do we have to make a Freedom of Information Act request?"

"MOM-MY!" Raven slapped a glare on Dell that made her sister flinch. "Mind your business, smelly Delly! At least I'm not an anorexic bone queen!"

"That's enough out of both of you! I swear, you children

giving me a pressure attack with your bickering. Dell Rae, you know better than to be bothering your sister when she's down about that job and everything else. Can't even act civilized at a nice Sunday dinner. I don't want to hear another peep out of either one of you."

"Peep," whispered Dell.

Gwen rolled her eyes at her, but didn't say anything. Raven stomped over to the refrigerator and angrily snatched at the metal ice tray stuck to the freezer. Smokey thumped on his tray and kicked his legs. Dell sat, quiet and uneasy. Why did she always have to fly off at the mouth, push too hard, win? She had meant to bring good news for Raven but instead had let her anger slip out. And the worst thing was that she wasn't even mad at Raven, not really. It was Raven's . . . predicament . . . that upset her. She was sad seeing Raven chained to a baby, but her feelings always came out mean. What should she do now?

She pulled Smokey from his high chair and stood him on the table. He smiled and squatted on his bowed legs. Then he started bouncing in rhythm as Dell sang.

"Cat named Mickey doin' that monkey, lum dee lum dee lie eye!"

Up and down, up and down bounced Smokey on his rubber legs. A gurgling sound sputtered from his drooling, toothless baby mouth. Raven was still sulking and fought off a smile. Smelly Delly made her sick. Bone queen.

Smokey said "aarrghkk."

Raven laughed.

He followed that up with "kkkkeeee."

Gwen smiled, grabbing hold of Smokey's dimpled hands and clapping them to the beat.

"Come on and do it, Mickey's Monkey, do it!" she sang.

Things were all right again. Dell decided it was time to tell the family about her plan to get Raven into college.

re you completely bugged?" Raven couldn't believe what her sister had just said.

"And why not?" protested Dell. "You read all the time and your grades were good."

"Read my lips, Dell, I can't spell. Mommy, remember the time I came home from school crying—I think I was in the fourth grade—because I failed the spelling test? I spelled 'saddle' with one *d*."

"Dell, your sister's right. That's the one subject she struggled with all through school. I don't want my baby to get her hopes up in a situation where she's bound to fail. Not everyone's like you. I'm with Raven on this one."

Raven didn't like that "not everyone's like you" bit, but was happy whenever her mother took her side against Dell.

"Now who wants some of the most golden-crusted, sweetest-appled pie this side of Brooklyn?"

Dell drifted into the rich aroma of cooked apples. "Hmmm,

yesss," she said, forgetting her mission for a moment. She held each bite in her mouth, luxuriously, chewed slowly, then sighed.

Raven chewed slowly too, thinking. Spelling, of all things. It was a stupid idea, and kind of mean. Dell probably wanted to make a fool of her because she was still furious she'd had a baby. Well, she didn't do it on purpose!

"I can't believe how negative you two are," complained Dell. "That's why we never get anywhere, because we're afraid to try."

"We who?" asked Raven.

"We project people. Black people. The poor. Anybody born outside society's charmed circle."

Raven did the eyebrow thing like Dell. "Boy, that's a change-up. Weren't you just calling us all homeys, hoodlums, and roughnecks? Now you're the big revolutionary."

"C'mon, you know I didn't mean it. Ai's all right, even if she does have that project booty."

"Mommy!"

"All right, all right. I'm joking. Listen, Rave, if you win the spelling bee you automatically get into an eight-week college prep program. Not only do they pay for college, they give you tutorial support, if you need it. Leah told me about it—her father's on the board. You want to stay in these projects all your life on public assistance, a *recipient*? Think about it at least. The test isn't until late June. You'd have plenty of time to prepare."

Gwen shook her head. "Now you know your mother's no

college graduate or nothing like that but I do have my share of common sense, and something tells me being a good speller don't mean you'll be good in all your other subjects. It's not right to get people thinking they can do this and that when . . ."

"But that's the whole idea, Mother. If people believe or even hope they can accomplish something they sure have a better chance than if they just resign themselves to fate. Look at you, you raised us, got your diploma, a good job. You didn't give up because some random bum left you in . . ."

"Dell Rae, don't talk about your father like that."

Dell raised her hands to her head. "*Omigod!* I have a father?! Why didn't anyone tell me? Li'l sis, we have a DADDY!"

As long as they were off the topic of college Raven was happy. She started singing her favorite R. Kelly song. "Any man can make a baby . . . but it takes a real man . . . to be a father . . ."

Dell offered a song of her own, sung in a deep, mocking voice: "Sometimes . . . I feel . . . like a fatherless child . . . he left us . . . aloooone . . . that bum left us . . . alone."

Gwen slapped the table. "Dell, I'm not saying it again! He's still your father and deserves respect. Since when is it a child's place to judge their parent, bum or not? Right up until the day he died, I never bad-mouthed my papa. But you two Supremes go right ahead and keep on singing. I'll tell you one thing, though, you need to count your blessings instead of complaining. The way half these men are out here today a lot of girls with daddies *at home* would gladly change places with you

46

knuckleheads. Just be thankful you not an outright, throwed-away orphan. You got me." Her voice cracked.

Dell and Raven leapt from their chairs, squealing, "No, Mama, no! Don't put us in no orphanage! Mama!" and grabbing hold of their mother's knees.

Smokey banged on his chair, all spit bubbles and giggles.

"Getting back to reality," Dell said. Raven groaned. "The spelling bee isn't only about spelling. The main purpose is to measure drive and discipline, to see if the person has heart. The prep program is where the real work comes in."

Gwen still had her doubts. "I just don't want to see your sister hurt."

Raven had stopped listening to their conversation and started up one of her own. "Whatever. Mommy, this is the bee-a-zest apple pie . . . can the baby have a tiny piece?"

"Raven, you know no little baby can't be eating no pie."

Dell's eyebrow shot up. "That Mrs. Jefferson, isn't she amazing, folks?! She can squeeze more double negatives into one sentence . . ." Raven and Gwen ignored Dell.

"Goody. More for me," said Raven, cutting off another hefty wedge.

Dell glanced at the pie plate and shrieked. "Stop eating all the pie before you explode. Mother, look at her, she's scarfing pie while we're talking!"

Gwen pushed the pie away from Raven. "I swear, you children driving me out my mind."

47

Raven yawned. "Well, you know what they say, a mind is a terrible thing to waste." She'd eaten three slices and each one tasted better than the other.

"Yeah," said Dell, "and a waist is a terrible thing to waste too, and yours seems to be vanishing faster than the Brazilian rain forest."

Raven slowly licked her lips. "Whatever."

10

aven lay in bed, listening. Her heart's beat, the baby's breathing, her mother's snores. It would be nice if those were the only sounds you heard at night. But somebody was playing music extra loud. A truck rumbled along the street. *I'm with Raven on this one.* The memory of those words brought a smile. She knew her mother loved her but it seemed like she was always comparing her to Dell. *Not everyone's like you.* Raven made a face. What did that mean? Maybe she couldn't spell that great but when they both were in school all her other grades were better than Dell's. Sure, Dell helped Mommy out with money when she needed it and Smokey was another mouth to feed. But Raven knew she could find a job. Maybe Aisha was right about her being too choosy. A bad memory returned. *It goes without saying that you need a diploma to get a job, any job. A job, any job.* She read again the piece of paper folded on the nightstand: "Spell Success and Go to College!" Dell had left the application under the pie plate.

Raven folded it in half, pushed it under her pillow, and clicked off the dim light. I better take whatever job I can get. With no diploma, who am I kidding that I can get an office job? Tomorrow's Monday. Get up early. Me and Aisha and the kids'll go . . . She dropped down into a heavy sleep.

Raven was flying, flying, carried on the wind like a stringless kite. Above the clouds, looking down at the City, speeding through New York's sky. It was so easy, effortless, no need to flap her winglike arms, she was coasting. Her flight carried her over bridges stretched like ribbons between boroughs, boats skimming rivers like speeding fish, twin silver skyscrapers, the Empire State Building, Central Park's oblong patch of green . . . Manhattan shimmered in light, and Raven owned it all.

Slowly, a heaviness began pulling at her. Was it around her waist? No, it was in the hips. She is falling, now inside a cloud bank, now below clouds, lower and lower, ever lower. What's happening? Raven is growing heavier by the second, weighed down, sinking. A glance back over her shoulder brings a shriek. Her butt is four times its normal size, a bulbous mound of flesh wide enough to fill the perimeter of a hula-hoop. Butt first, Raven plunges, like a lead ball thrown from a rooftop. A shock, then stillness.

There's Dell, shaking her head, holding a death certificate. "I told her, I told her." She fills in the "Cause of Death" blank: *Project Booty.*

11

fried food had always tasted extra good to Raven. She loved it, fried potatoes, fried chicken, fried bologna, fried okra, fried anything. Not anymore. Not since she took the job at Catfish Corner. Thanks to Aisha, who had pointed out the small sign to her on their way to the mall. "Now Hiring for Part-time and Full-time Positions. No Diploma Needed." "Why not check it out, Rave? It might be phat, especially if me and Star get some freebies."

That was five weeks ago. It already felt like five years. Dell was right. It is a bad sign when they want you to start work right then and there. Slave labor, she'd said.

"Can I take your order?" Raven forced a smile as she said that for the umpteenth time, then waited. She couldn't understand why the same people who came in every day for lunch had to spend so much time staring at the menu. It wasn't as if it ever changed. And they always ended up ordering the same thing they usually got anyway.

Or why anyone would even bother asking, like the old church ladies did, "Honey, your fish fresh?" What'd they think? Of course it wasn't fresh. This was a fast-food joint on a crowded side street in the middle of Brooklyn, not some fancy restaurant in the City. The catfish came frozen in crates from God-knows-where and sat in stacks in basement freezers for God-knows-how-long. But in orientation she was told to answer, "As fresh as a newborn's smile." So she did.

"What a sweet way to put it, bless your little heart. In that case I'll have the jumbo platter to go."

At least she finally had a job. The pay wasn't great—she worked only three hours a day, during the 11-to-2 lunch-hour rush—but it was enough to keep Smokey fed and diapered without having to bug Mommy for money. Raven tried to explain it exactly that way but Mommy had only one thing to say—she didn't want her working in that grease pit. And Dell just kept repeating "slave wages for slave labor."

Aisha was really into Raven's new job, most of all when she showed up with the kids and Raven loaded their plates with extras. And she didn't mind babysitting since the Jeffersons had cable, but she'd had to promise not to let any more "visitors" drop by.

Raven was at the end of her shift. A customer walked up as she tallied her register's lunchtime take.

"Sorry, I'm closed," she said, glancing up, kind of annoyed. Her jaw dropped but no sound came out. Her eyes blinked but the green-eyed ghost didn't vanish. Her face got hot.

"Raven! How're you doing? I meant to call you but . . ." The boy didn't finish his sentence. He looked much taller than she'd remembered him, and more grown. The boy started fidgeting.

"You *do* remember me, right? The party in Hillbrook Houses . . . Jeez, when was that? Let me see . . . a year ago . . . Hillbrook, that's the name of your projects, right? I remember thinking how funny that was, a place called Hillbrook with no hills or brooks. Maybe you don't remember . . ."

"I remember you, Jesse. It's just that . . . I didn't think I'd ever . . . you caught me by surprise, that's all." His face brightened. She remembered his name.

"How long've you been working here? You like it? I thought you were at Franklin High. I used to eat lunch here all the time, then I switched when that new place opened up across the way, the Burger Pit. But I don't know, something told me to come in here today. And look who's here. Destiny, huh?"

Raven was embarrassed about her job. "I've only been here a few weeks. It's temporary, you know, only for now. I had an interview the other day with this insurance company and I'm waiting to hear . . ."

A million thoughts were swirling in Raven's mind. This was Smokey's father, yet she knew so little about him, not even his last name. And he didn't even know their baby existed. They were connected in a big way, but they were strangers. Sure they'd talked and talked at the party but now all she could remember was that he was nice-looking and she'd liked him and everything had seemed so amazing, how they got along right away and . . .

What else did she remember? He was eighteen, went to Stevenson High School, and lived with his mother and father. She didn't know many kids who had both parents at home and had been impressed, like Jesse must've deserved it, for doing something right or being something good.

Why hadn't he called? Mommy had said, "Don't sit by the phone like a fool, child. That boy done gone off on his merry way. Believe you me, I have been there and back. Twice. At least I *knew* your father, had been with him for years. Well, off and on. Not that he turned out to be worth a damn, but still . . . Mark my words, Raven, your best bet is to put that boy out of your mind before you end up with a half dozen more mouths to feed." Mommy had been so absolute, that it made what she was saying sound right.

Everything was so confusing. Part of her was still mad and hurt, and part of her was happy to see him. It wasn't like he *knew* and then dissed her. He never had the chance to . . . to what? Marry her, a girl he didn't even know? Be a father to his son, a baby he might not even want?

"Raven, is your register done? Flirting's on your own time." The manager's voice.

"Yeah, I'm finished, Miss Bert," she answered, sticking the tally card in the register and shutting the cash drawer.

Jesse pulled at the brim of his Knicks cap. "Hey, if you're getting off work now, maybe we could go over to the Pit and hang out. No lie, I intended to call."

12

ll the schools in the area had emptied out directly into the
Burger Pit. Kids squeezed around tables and shouted
orders to their friends on line. Boys shoved each other
against girls and were met with kicks and "Get away from me!"
Textbooks, spiral notebooks, leather bags, and cloth knapsacks
were scattered and stacked all about. The scene reminded
Raven of her life before Jesse. He appeared at the table with a
tray.

"Two vanilla milk shakes coming up, ma'am, straight out
the cow."

"Thanks." Raven didn't remember Jesse being so lame.
Straight out the cow. Where'd he get that, *Beavis and Butt-
Head*? At the party, he'd eased up and whispered in her ear,
"What up, sister, waiting for me? 'Cause ya know I been steady
scopin' you from a distance. Can I get that name?" A few days
later, she was listening to a Keith Sweat CD at Aisha's and heard
him singing the same thing. She should've known then that

something was not quite straight up with Jesse, that he wouldn't call.

They sat facing each other. Raven saw again those dreamy eyes. Jesse's straw made a loud sucking noise. He giggled.

"Excuuuuse me." He smacked his lips. "Hmmm, they do milk shakes right!" She tried to imagine this boy, Smokey's father, as her husband, her man. She couldn't. He didn't even look like a man, with that baby fuzz mustache.

"So, Jesse, what's your last name?"

"We never did get to all that, did we? Honoré. My great-grands were from Haiti. What's yours?"

"Jefferson. My great-grands were from Plantation."

"Where?"

"Thomas Jefferson's slave plantation. Everybody knows he has a bunch of black people in his family." They laughed into their straws, then couldn't find anything else to say. So they sat with the straws in their mouths.

Jesse came up with "So what you been up to? How's school?"

"I left."

"You're kidding, Raven, no way! I thought you were planning on college. Wow. You didn't seem, you know, like the type."

"What type?"

"Well, you know, the dropout type. You seemed kind of different."

"Different from what, Jesse?"

"I don't know, from kids who drop out of school."

"And you could tell all this about me from that one time we . . . uh . . . met." Heat flooded her cheeks.

"Uh-huh. Jeez, my folks would have my rear if I tried to pull something like that. For me, it's college or else. Why'd you quit?"

Raven stirred the vanilla foam in the bottom of her cup. "I had a baby."

Jesse's eyes opened wide. He knew so many girls who got themselves "in the family way," as his mother put it. He felt sorry for her.

"Wow, that's deep. You getting married or what?"

"Nope. The father never called."

Jesse squinted, like he was trying to bring her into focus. His eyes stayed that way for a long time. Raven kept stirring her shake. Then he said, "Hey, come on, that's not funny."

"I know it's not. You have a four-month-old son."

"*What?!* But I'm only fifteen and a half!"

A group of kids at another table looked over at them, laughed, and resumed talking.

Jesse was whispering now. "Raven, how do you know it's . . . that I'm the . . . ?"

"Jesse!" She lowered her voice. "It was my first time. My only time."

"But you said you'd done it before."

"And *you* said you were *eighteen*."

Jesse slumped back and blew hard, like he was blowing out a candle. "I can't believe this. I'm a daddy? What am I going to tell my dad?" He stirred the vanilla foam and stirred it some more. Raven did too.

Aisha put that certain look on her face when she heard Raven's keys rattle. Raven was not one, not one and a half, but *two* hours late. No big deal, really. Smokey hadn't cried once and Starlett had played with all his baby stuff while Aisha watched TV and talked on the phone. But since Rave always gave *her* the look when *she* messed up, she was going to do the same thing. On general principle. Aisha, all frown and primped lips, stood posed at the table with a finger pointing at the kitchen clock when Raven rushed in.

"We have to talk. The baby okay? Aisha, I don't know what to do, whether I'm coming or going. What time is it? Four-thirty?! I didn't know it was so late. Sorry, Ai. But when I tell you what happened you're gonna flip. Okay, okay, four-thirty . . . so that means Mommy's going to be home in an hour. I have to get myself together. What should I do?"

Aisha dropped her pose. "How *I* know? I don't even know why you buggin' in the first place."

Raven told her the story.

"Fifteen? He looked like a full-grown man at the party, like he played ball for the NBA or something. And you say he only fifteen?"

"And a half," said Raven, bouncing Starlett on her knees.

The little girl put her face against Raven's uniform. "Fench fie, Mama! Fench fie!"

Aisha pulled her daughter onto her own lap. "Star, you'll get french fries at home. Now be quiet." She thought a minute. "Yeah, that 'half' part shows right there that he nothin' but a child. That would be like us saying we seventeen going on eighteen. Still, if he nice and he into you, check him out some more and see what the deal is. Just don't play yourself, you know, acting all desperate like 'Please help me and my baby,' 'cause he will definitely step. Be chill, like hey, I'm a mother now and I'm ready to deal with the real. Then they don't feel like you sweatin' 'em. So what if he corny. I wish all these boys were more corny and less horny. And Smokey should have his daddy around. I was mad when you said that thing about Starlett's father never being here with us, but it's true."

"I'm sorry, Aisha. I shouldn't have gone there. I know you're right about Smokey needing a father. I wish I'd had one. But first, I know next to nothing about him, second, he's more of a baby than me, and third, I don't know if he even wants to be in our life. Mommy said these boys out here don't even know how to spell responsibility."

"I'm not sayin' y'all have to get married and stuff. Look at it this way: He in school, right? He live at home and ain't runnin' the streets, right? His folks got the cash, right? He got plans for the future, right? So how you know, he might be different."

Almost to herself, Raven said, "That's what he'd thought about me."

Aisha stood to leave. "It's a trip but don't stress it. See what he say, and if it sound good, go for it. I'm down to be the maid of honor. But right now, me and my hungry child gots to go. Come on, Star, we go get you some fench fie."

Raven was by herself. She went to the back room where her baby had been sleeping. He was awake in his crib. At the sight of her, he broke into a broad, pink-gummed grin. She pressed him against her chest. "Is that a smile I see? Huh? Is that a smile? Happy to have a daddy? Yes, he sure is, Smokey's happy to have a daddy."

13

This time, he did call. It was ten in the morning. Raven had Smokey cuddled in her lap and was reading *Green Eggs and Ham* to him. She could tell he liked Dr. Seuss stories by the way he slapped at the pages when she read. With her free hand she reached for the phone.

"Hello . . . hello?"

There was a pause, then "Is that him, Raven? Is that him in the background? Wow!"

"Jesse?"

"I still can't believe it. I was so, like, I don't know, dumbfounded when you told me about the baby that I forgot to ask his name. What'd you name him?"

"Smokey. My mother chose it."

"Smokey, hmmm, it's nice, yeah, Smokey Jefferson."

"Why not Smokey Honoré?"

"Okay, yeah, Smokey Honoré. Cool. Listen up. I've been thinking about you and him and me and everything all day and night and day. I'm between classes and gotta run but I thought that if you're working today maybe I could meet you afterward and come see your baby. I mean, my . . . I mean the . . ."

Raven wanted to leap and shriek and dance. Mommy said "no company" but this was different, Jesse might be her future son-in-law!

"Okay. I get off at two."

Raven's last customer was asking for extra hot sauce when Jesse walked in, waved, and sat down. Miss Bert eyed him, then Raven, but said nothing. Raven felt shy and wished she didn't smell fried. On the way to the bus stop they made small talk.

There were only two kids in Jesse's family too. He had an older sister in college. His mother was a lawyer who worked for herself and his father was principal of a high school. "*My* high school," complained Jesse. They lived in the Clinton Hill area over by Prospect Park. Raven told him about her mother and Dell and her hope to go back to school.

"You *should*, Raven. I feel like it's my fault too, you know what I mean, like it shouldn't be just on you."

The bus arrived. Like any other pair of high schoolers, they showed their bus passes to the driver and found seats.

"Really, my dad could probably hook you up with a different high school. He knows everything about schools."

"So you told your folks about Smokey?"

"Nah . . . uh . . . but I will. Probably tomorrow."

Raven almost said "yeah, right" but didn't. *Just be chill.*

"Don't feel guilty. I got myself in this situation. And you don't have to do anything for me. I'm a mother now and I'm ready to deal with the real." *Don't play yourself.*

From the living-room window, Aisha spotted Raven and Jesse stepping from the bus. She watched them enter the building, then ran up the hallway and listened with her ear pressed against the door. At the sound of Raven's voice, she dashed over to Smokey's bassinet and adjusted his new outfit one last time. She positioned him the way Raven said she should. The key turned inside the last lock. She planted Starlett on the couch, snatched up a magazine, and tried to look like she was deep into it when Raven walked in, followed by Jesse.

The baby instantly caught Jesse's eye. "Hey . . . check out the little man!" He scooped him up. "Well, look at you Mr. Smokey. Wassup?" He lifted his son over his head. "I cannot believe this! He even looks like me!"

"Well . . . ," began Aisha, but Raven shut her up with a glance.

"Aisha, Jesse. Jesse, Aisha. She's my best friend. And that's Starlett, Ai's little girl."

"Hey. Say 'wassup,' Smokey. C'mon, give the ladies a 'wassup.' Wassup, wassup, wassup."

Raven and Aisha exchanged smiles.

Aisha took Starlett's hand. "Peace, we outta here. Check you later. Nice meeting you, Jesse."

Raven locked the door and Jesse lifted Smokey up and down like a barbell. She went to change out of her work clothes. In her room she whispered to the mirror, "Looking good." Her stomach was full of butterflies.

Smokey was flying like Superboy, his chubby cheeks red with excitement. A splat of baby drool landed on Jesse's forehead.

"Whoa, my man . . . uh, Raven . . ."

Raven took the baby and slipped a pacifier between his gums. "We got grape soda. Want some?"

"No Coke? Okay, grape's all right. Is it safe to hold him again?" The plastic couch cover wheezed when Jesse sat down.

Raven placed Smokey on his daddy's knees. "You don't have a thing to worry about as long as you keep him sea level." What a picture. The same full lips, the same high forehead, the same hazel eyes. She went to the kitchen and returned with the cold can of soda.

Jesse made a fake coughing sound, then said, "Uh, I have to confess something. I told you a lie."

"Another one? What, you're really not fifteen and a half?"

"Nah, nah, not that. I'm definitely fifteen and a half. I lied when I said I didn't tell my folks. I did. Right away. My mom always knows when something's going on anyway and she can get everything out of me."

"And?" Raven could tell it wasn't going to be good.

Bouncing Smokey on his knees, Jesse explained himself. "Well, my folks are very conservative and they almost had a cow. I thought my dad was going to deck me. He said I might as well pack my bags if I thought I was bringing home . . . you know . . . a project baby. Mother kept saying they had worked too long, that they weren't going to let me ruin my life, you know, yelling and all. But don't get me wrong, I want to be a father to my son, no doubt about it. I'm definitely going to do the right thing, you know, birthdays, Christmas, help you guys out with money when I can. Definitely. I just can't do much more right now. You know how it is—parents rule."

Raven took her baby from the boy and cradled him. "Parents rule? Jesse, you're a parent now too. Rule yourself. So all of a sudden me and Smokey are 'you guys,' like we're on our own and you're wishing us good luck?"

"That's not what I . . ."

"Jesse you don't have to say it. I should've known, I should've known. Mommy was so right, you're all just little boys who can't even spell responsibility. This is what I don't get, Jesse. Why'd you even bother coming to see *your son*? To make sure he looked like you? Or did you just want to do the right thing, because if that's the reason, don't bother, it's not Christmas yet."

"Aw, come on, Raven, why you gotta go there?"

"I'm not going anywhere. You are. I'll let you out. I can't have company when Mommy's at work."

Raven slumped in a corner of the couch. *A project baby.* On the television a woman was taking a swing at a talk-show host. How could Smokey's own grandparents be so heartless? She sat and thought and thought some more. Then she just sat. Empty. She didn't hear the door open.

"You didn't hear me calling to you, Raven? That TV got you

in a trance. I don't know how you can watch that nonsense. The guests on those shows are only half as crazy as the ones who go dig them up in the first place."

Gwen sat down and untied her shoes. Raven was still seething. Smokey didn't need any stuck-up, put-the-B-in-bourgeois, snobby grandparents anyhow.

"And how was your day?"

"Just like this."

"No visitors, I hope." Raven burst into tears. "Lord, child, what's wrong?!" Gwen rushed over and took her in her arms. "The baby hurt?" Raven could only shake her head. She was sobbing too much to say words. She let herself sink deeper in her mother's embrace, crying like she had years earlier when Dell threw her black Cabbage Patch doll in the incinerator with the trash, supposedly by accident.

When the sobbing stopped, Gwen took Raven's face in her hands. "Now tell me what on earth they've done to my baby." She listened, shaking her head slowly, as Raven told her about the baby's father showing up at her job, their talk at the Burger Pit, his visit, what he said, what he said his parents said, the whole story. Except the part about his age. That was just too embarrassing.

"Mommy, I know you're through with me . . . that I let you down. You used to be proud of me too . . . I remember you used to say I might go farther than Dell, maybe to a four-year college. Look at me now, a baby, no serious job, no future, a bur . . ." "Burden" didn't make it out of her mouth. Again, she sank into her mother and cried from that deep place.

They stayed wrapped like that for a good while. Raven wiped her nose on the sleeve of her blouse. Her mother's eyes were shiny and wet. "Baby, don't mess up your nice top." Gwen pulled a handful of tissues from a box and dabbed at Raven's cheeks and nose. It was funny, the things that sprang into your head at the strangest moments. She flashed on Raven the toddler, snatching her head from side to side while Gwen begged her to "let Mommy wipe your nose, be a good girl." But her grown-up Raven let her do it. Children were something else again. "Sweetie, don't ever say I'm through with you. I'm your mother and you're my baby daughter. And I *am* proud of you, yes I am, seeing you learning to be a mother to Smokey, struggling to find your way again. And you gave me a beautiful grandchild. I love you so much, Raven. I might not always show it the way I should but . . ." The words stopped coming.

She *had* been tough with Raven, as though she was trying to punish her own self. Raven's "problem" had taken her thoughts back to those bad times she wanted to forget. "I tried to protect you girls, keep you from making the same mistakes I did at your age . . . but I failed. Maybe I seem mad at you but I'm really mad at myself." Raven wasn't used to them talking this way. It felt almost like being with Aisha, getting your deep-down feelings out, telling the truth.

"You didn't fail anybody, Mommy. I didn't 'think first, act second' like you always told me. Then when Jesse showed up I had this fantasy he would swoop down like something from heaven and make everything right again."

Gwen nodded. "That's a fantasy I know all too well. Let me

tell you something, woman to woman. No man's about to save you or me or Dell or anybody. You know that saying: sooner or later every man starts barking? Not that I'm saying all men are dogs. It just takes a whole lotta searching to find one who can spell . . ."

". . . responsibility," they said together.

Raven thought about what she should do but no answers came. "I still feel like I'm back to nowhere."

"No Jefferson is ever nowhere. Let your mother tell you what you're gonna do. You will keep taking good care of my grandchild, quit that hot-grease-spitting job, and get back to your books. You can't start all over again but you can sure pick up where you left off."

14

At first Aisha thought the wall paint at Raven's was peeling. Strips dangled near the sink, above the TV, in the hall, everywhere. She couldn't quite believe her eyes.

"Have you snapped, Rave, completely cracked?"

Raven looked proudly at the walls covered with scribbled slips of paper. Each had a word she'd copied out of the dictionary. She was up to the *e*'s.

"No doubt about that. I know it looks strange but I am definitely going to improve my spelling so I can go to college. But first I have to win a spelling bee. Dell told me about it."

Aisha stepped closer to a wall. "Dell. Hmmmph. Another bookworm. She so nerdy it's like she not even from the projects. Don't pull on 'em, Star." Starlett stuck "e-r-r-a-t-i-c" on her cheek. Aisha moved her away from the wall, then eased closer herself. "Let me see this . . . a-bo . . . a-blow . . . I can't even say these words."

"That's 'ablution,'" said Raven, closing her eyes, "a-b-l-u-t-i-o-n." The girls slapped each other five.

"Go, Rave! You know what all these words mean?"

"Nope. Don't have to. Just gotta spell them right."

Aisha shook her head. "Well, more power to you, Miss Jefferson. All I know is that by the time you memorize every word in that dictionary, you *will* be Raven. A ravin' lunatic. The brain wasn't meant to hold but so much. You ready?"

"Yeah, let's hit it." Raven took Smokey from the crib and sat him in his stroller.

"Red?" asked Aisha, eyeing the baby's outfit.

"That's right! The sun is shining and the Jeffersons are feeling good. Right, Smokee-kee?" She kissed her son's face. "I'm bringing my cards." Aisha glanced at Raven's "Improve Your Spelling" flash cards.

"What kind of cards is that? We not playing knucks?"

"Nope. You hit too hard. My knuckles are all scarred up from playing knucks with you. These are word cards. You have to test me when we get outside, all right?"

Aisha moaned.

The elevator squeaked and stopped. Aisha yanked open the heavy door, because if you didn't open it fast the elevator would take off and be gone. Two girls she didn't recognize, wearing blond extensions in their hair and baggy, matching sweatshirts, were standing smack in the middle of the floor. Mrs. Hendricks was leaning against the wall. And in a corner was that fine-looking Arkim from the fourteenth floor with his scary pit bull. Good thing Arkim's legs always held the dog tight in a corner. Aisha didn't like animals.

Raven tried pushing the stroller into the elevator. "Excuse me, excuse me." One of the blondes groaned. The other one made a long drawn-out sucking sound. They didn't move.

"Y'all just gon' have to wait for the next one! Ain't no room for no big honkin' carriage," said one.

"And ya know that! And it's hot up in here too. Unh-unh, not today, José," added the other. Aisha sized up the situation. They were little wannabes. Skanks. Toothpicks.

"Rave, hold Star's hand for me." Aisha switched places with her friend, turned the stroller around, and backed her one-hundred-seventy-pound self into the elevator.

"Ouch, you crushing my foot! And get your big butt outta my stomach. Y'all act like this the last elevator in life."

"Word up! Just 'cause they got them babies they think everybody suppose to make way. A baby don't make you special. Y'all need to wait your two-tons-of-fun asses for another elevator." The blondes kept mumbling and moaning behind Aisha's crushing frame.

"Get in, girls," announced Ai, "there's mucho room now." Raven and Starlett squeezed in. Aisha looked the girls, who'd been forced to move to the side, dead in their faces. "Y'all do *not* live in Hillbrook Houses. *We* do. Our rent pay for these elevators. And if your bony analrexic tails got something to say about it, then let's get it on, we ready to throw down right here, right now. And when we do, this *will* be *your* last elevator in life. Now, who got something else to say . . . *José?*"

The only sound heard on the ride down was an urgent "Lord have mercy" from Mrs. Hendricks.

Raven and Aisha were still howling as they sat down on the bench at the concrete checker tables. Sunshine glinted off building windows. Smokey sucked on a pacifier and Starlett watched an ant crawling across her hand. Music could be heard from people's apartments. Raven bounced to the beat. She liked that about the projects, everybody grooving to the same tunes. But being outside was one thing. When she was upstairs with the baby and somebody's bomb bass was pounding the walls, that was a drag. Sometimes she couldn't even fall asleep. Right then, though, hanging with Aisha and the kids, everything was how she liked it.

Aisha jumped to her feet. "Owww, Mary J. is da bomb!" She broke out singing and dancing, her big body in sync with the rhythm. "I'm like them church ladies. When the spirit move you, you gotta move with it." Smokey was twisting and Starlett was singing, "Mama! Mama!" Raven closed her eyes and tuned out everything but the soulful voice of Mary J. Blige. She was happy.

"Ai, I have to give it to you, you sure read their beads, I mean you read them *for days.*" Not being much of a fighter herself, she admired how Ai was always ready to throw down.

"Them girls was so *tired.* Then they gonna cop attitude. I heard that in the olden days if you had a baby or were pregnant or something people would give you their seat on the subway and hold doors for you and everything."

72

"Ai, they didn't *have* subways in the olden days."

"Well, whatever, you know what I mean, they'd stop the horse so you could cross the road. But not no more."

Arkim walked up, holding a red, black, and green leash. "What's happenin', honeys? Y'all met my dog Homey, right?" Homey was busy with Starlett, shimmying and pushing his head into her hand.

Aisha's eyes got big and she drew her thick legs close to her body. "Don't touch it, Star!" Starlett grinned, rubbing the puppy's soft fur.

"Aw, Homey wouldn't hurt nobody. He still a baby, not even three months old. I'm not scared of your babies, so don't be scared of mine."

Aisha wasn't having it. "Yeah, but our babies don't bite. Starlett, get over here." The dog was licking Starlett's palm.

"Ai, don't make her afraid of dogs just because you are," warned Raven. "That's how parents mess up their kids, teaching them by their bad example."

"So what about that dog in Florida that jumped over the fence and bit this baby up so bad . . ."

"Homey! Come." The puppy scrambled over to Arkim and flopped down across his basketball shoe. "See. He's a good dog. Hey, I like how y'all did them fake blondies in the elevator. Them lame folks from Fort Crusty *need* to get dogged. Check y'all later. "

Starlett waved her wet hand. "Bye-bye, dog."

Aisha relaxed. "Excuse me, but I don't like no kinda dog getting near me or my daughter. That pit bull in Florida . . ."

Raven didn't want Aisha to go into the whole gross story. She was eager to practice her spelling. "I saw that on the news too. But that was one dog."

"Oh. Like the rest of them are all friendly like Beethoven in that movie. You do what you like but me and my child keeping our distance. Star, no doggie, no! Doggie bad."

Starlett smiled at her hand.

Aisha slapped herself on the forehead. "Oh, yeah! What I was saying about people letting you cross the street in the olden days was that my girl Natalia, you know her, they call her Ta-Ta and she live in the building next to the cleaners, she got a purple birthmark on her cheek, or whatever that thing is . . ."

Raven looked to the sky like she was praying for mercy. "Yes, Aisha, I know Natalia Williams." Aisha pretended to ignore Raven's tone of voice.

"Well, she told me that this girl she know, seven months pregnant, was crossing the street down on De Kalb in all this crazy traffic . . ."

"Is it something horrible? You know I don't like horror stories."

"It ain't all that, Rave. Chill. So Natalia had said . . . By the way, did you hear they trying to put her family out the projects 'cause her brother got busted with . . ."

"Just tell me about the pregnant girl, Aisha. How many times do I have to tell you to get to the point, Poindexter. I hate the way you tell stories."

"Okay! So she—I think her name was Glenda—so Glenda

was in the middle of all this crazy traffic and—I couldn't believe this, I was like, 'Nooo.' Well, a cop stopped his car, got out, and made the cars stop so this Glenda girl could get across the street. Ain't that a trip? A cop."

Raven didn't see the big deal. All cops weren't bad. But the only way she could get them going on her words was to join in with Aisha's amazement. "That *is* something. Okay, time for my words." Raven pulled out the box of flash cards and placed it in front of Aisha.

Aisha pushed the cards away. "Wait a minute, hold up. You never gave me the 411 on what happened with Jesse. How did all that shake out?"

"Oh, him. He's a boy who can't spell responsibility, that's what happened. I mean, I guess I still like him but he's too young and immature to be a daddy. Plus, his folks are against us being together, even if there was a chance. You know the type, wannabe bourgeois Huxtables, their precious boy too good for a project girl. I cried my head off about it with Mommy . . ."

"With your moms?! That's raw."

"Yeah, I know. I feel like we got closer. Now I'm concentrating on taking care of myself and my baby. I'll just be a single mother like everybody else. Strong with or without a man."

"Word up, I hear that."

"Anyway, sooner or later, every man starts barking. That's what Mommy says."

Aisha was surprised. "Miss Jefferson say it too? I got that from *my* moms."

Raven raised her eyebrows. "How funny! What do they call that again? The oral tradition."

"The what?"

"Never mind, Aisha. Now can we do my cards?"

Raven pushed the box across the table a second time. "I have to learn all of these. You say the word out loud. I spell it. Then you tell me if I'm right or wrong."

"I don't know about all this. You used to wanna do fun things. I *told* you I can't say these words."

"Just try. Read me the definition in case I don't understand your pronunciation."

"Ah-ight. The first word is sub . . . sutt . . . It mean delicate. Like me."

"S-u-t-t-l-e. I mean, e-l."

"Nope. S-u-b-t-l-e."

"Dag! That's a bad start. What's next?"

"Eni-gam. No . . . ma."

"What?"

"Umm, engama . . . Shoot, I don't know. It say, obsker."

"Aisha, what are you talking about? Gimme the card!" Raven snatched it. "It's enigma, e-n-i-g-m-a. Obscure. Like a riddle you can't figure out."

"You mean like your hairdo? Ha! No, all jokes aside, that don't count. You cheated."

"I did not! I had to look because you didn't say it right and I couldn't understand you."

"That's 'cause I'm too—what was it?—sub-tull for ya. Hey, hey, and ya *know* that."

They got through half the box. Raven was depressed about how many she got wrong, but like Aisha said, at least she got some right too. Nothing was going to make her change her mind, though, about taking the test. "Let's walk the bridge. I want to drop off this application at Dell's job. It's not far. She said it's down from City Hall. We'll surprise her." Aisha was game but only if they could stop first at J&R Music World to look at CDs. She'd gotten her public assistance check and was feeling rich.

15

A bell went "bing!" at the same time the number "20" lit up. The tall elevator doors slid open, smooth and silent. "Now *that's* a ride," said Raven, pushing the stroller past three men in sleek business suits.

"Now *that's* some benjamins," exclaimed Aisha, looking at the men. "They got nothin' *but* hundreds in their wallets." She was carrying a plastic shopping bag from J&R in one hand and leading Starlett with the other. The lawyers looked straight past them and boarded the elevator.

"How would you know if Benjamin Franklin's face is on a one-hundred-dollar bill? It's not like you've ever seen one," teased Raven. She compared the note in her hand to the gold-lettered name on the wall. "Baskerville, Farragut and Associates. Looks like we're in the right place."

"PEE-PEE!" yelled Starlett. The walk and shopping had tired her out. She was cranky. And Smokey had begun to whimper.

Raven felt the seat of his pants. "Uh-oh. Code red." The group headed for the reception area.

"I could sleep on this carpet," whispered Ai, "and I have too seen a hundred dollar bill. The only ones you ever seen is them fakes I slipped you at Catfish Corner."

The receptionist scrutinized them from behind dark oak. She had extensions like Aisha's but wore hers up in a bun. "Yes? Are you looking for . . . something?"

Aisha didn't like the look on her face when she said "something." "Yeah, where your baffroom?"

"I'm sorry but this is a private law office. There are public rest rooms down in the . . ."

Raven spoke up. "I'm Raven Jefferson. We're here to see my sister Dell Jefferson, the legal assistant."

"The paralegal? Please take a seat. I'll see if she's in." There was no mistaking her attitude; she thought she was better than them.

Aisha's nostrils flared. A bad sign. Raven gave her the Look and mouthed, "No." Too late.

"Let's get one thing straight, girlfriend. I don't know who told you your shit don't stink . . ."

The receptionist quickly rose to her feet. "Ex-cuse me?!"

"You *heard* me. Now where's the goddamn baffroom? You see we got crying kids with us. And they have to go!"

A woman stepped out from a side corridor. Her suit was like the ones worn by the men at the elevator, except she had a skirt. She stood nearly six feet tall and talked fast. "Brandy, we're going to need coffee for eight and tea for four in conference room B. Don't forget the milk and sugar. And tell Photo-copy to bring seven more sets of those real estate documents. Bound. Now, please." She glimpsed the black kids. "And please have your friends take a seat, my clients will be here any minute."

A pained look twisted the receptionist's face. "Certainly, Miss Wilson. These visitors are here for . . ." Before she could finish, the lawyer had hurried off. "The *rest rooms* are through that door," she said, pointing.

Aisha smiled. "Thank you. *Braaaan-deee.*" In the spacious, glistening bathroom, Aisha snorted the name. "Brandy. Right. She *wish* she look good as Brandy. Brandy is *fine.* I read in a magazine that she gonna model after she stop singing and doing her TV show."

"I can see her as a model, she's really pretty," added Raven. "What gets me is why do people have to get so stuck up because they have a good job? Brandy's a star but she's still down to earth. But that girl out there, what a joke. A job doesn't make you better than anybody else. People are so freak outside the projects. I have to say, even though she's my sister, that Dell can be like that too. Uppity."

"Word. That's why she don't really take to me. I'm probably too project for her too." They talked more, got Starlett and Smokey squared away, admired the gigantic mirrors, admired themselves in the mirrors, admired their kids in the mirrors, and marched out to meet Dell.

A pale, dark-haired young woman in a plain gray dress was waiting for them. "Hi! You must be Raven. I've heard a lot about you. And there's Smokey! Dell's always flashing his photo. At last I get to see him in person. He's precious. Dell's right, he *does* look like Smokey Robinson. My mother has all the old Miracles albums. And who's this little sweetheart? She looks sleepy. Did you miss your nap today? What a doll . . . and look at those adorable earrings. Oh, I'm sorry, I'm Leah, Dell's office mate. She's in a meeting right now but should be out shortly. She asked me to come get you guys." She held out her hand and shook Raven's, then Aisha's, then Starlett's. Then she wiggled Smokey's finger. She turned back to Aisha. "I'm sorry, I didn't get your name."

"Ai." Aisha wondered why white girls were always saying they were sorry about something.

"That's an interesting name. How's it spelled?"

"You are *not* going there too! I been doing spelling words all day!"

Raven busted out laughing. She explained to Leah how they had spent the morning. Leah laughed too.

"Well, let's go, guys, the paralegal pigpen is way at the end of the corridor." Aisha made a grunting noise as she passed by the reception desk. The receptionist did not look up. The troupe passed offices as big as apartments. Lawyers' eyes darted their way, then away.

"Here we are—Home Sweet Hell. Sit wherever you can."

The office for the two legal assistants was half the size of the lawyer offices, windowless, and had two small desks. There were boxes of papers, stacks of papers, and folders of papers all over. On the wall above Leah's desk was a poster of a cowboy with a guitar, a white ponytail, and an old face. "Willie Nelson—Singer, Songwriter" was printed across the bottom. Raven chuckled to herself, imagining Dell singing and Leah crying.

"You know, Raven, I'm really pleased you're thinking about doing the college prep program. Dell's been talking about it nonstop. She really, really wants you to."

Raven's stomach dropped. "Subtle" came to mind. She'd gotten it wrong the first time. S-u-b-t-l-e. "Well, I can't say for sure I'll be in the program. I'm going to try for the spelling bee. Then we'll see."

"You're too modest. I heard how bright you are. Don't waste it. Did you know that the wage gap between high school and college graduates is wider than ever? I'm sorry, but in this economy a high school diploma is total wishful thinking."

"Told you," said Aisha. "I *knew* school was a waste of my valuable time."

Leah sat on a box. "Nooo . . . *that's* not my point, Oy."

"Who Oy?" Ai frowned, but Leah didn't hear her.

"I'm saying a little bit of school won't get you far but a lot will take you straight to the top, inside the charmed circle."

Charmed circle. Raven thought she'd heard that before. She had! So *that's* where Dell got it, trying to make it seem like she came up with it herself.

"I'm planning to go back myself and get my law degree. Are you applying to Spell Success too?"

"No bout a-doubt it."

"I'm sorry, what'd you say?"

Raven answered for Aisha. "She said no doubt about it but she was kidding. She's not doing the test." Raven's thoughts were still in the earlier conversation. So Dell said good things about her and showed Smokey's picture to people at work. That was a nice thing to know. She sure didn't act like that at home, like she was proud of them.

Leah was a surprise too. She seemed friendly in a real way, not just trying to act nice because they were black. And Leah's mother sounded as if she was old school too, into the Miracles just like Mommy. She sure was nicer than that stuck-up receptionist. And *she* was black. What a bugged world. Sometimes it seemed like whatever you expected, the opposite happened.

"Can I hold the baby?" asked Leah, reaching for Smokey. She cooed in his ear.

Raven noticed a poster for the movie *Manhattan*. Leah followed Raven's eyes. "Did you see *Manhattan*? Woody Allen is so gifted, so wonderfully neurotic. I love him and I don't care a whit about his personal life. I guess I'm French that way. Do you like him?"

Aisha quickly turned away, mumbling something under her breath. Raven avoided the question. "You go to a lot of movies?"

"Are you kidding? I'm like a total movie fanatic. Everybody hates to go with me because I always cry. I even cried at *Babe*. Remember the part where Babe was in that dark pen with his brothers and sisters right after they had taken his mother off to the slaughterhouse and he said, 'I . . . want . . . my mommy,' and a tiny tear rolled down his snout? God, I thought I was going to lose it right there."

"I missed that one."

"You *must* see it, Raven. And you too, Oy. Starlett would *love* it. It has all these messages about prejudice and diversity. It's actually a film for adults in the guise of a children's movie. I bought it and watch it at home all the time. Maybe I'll have you guys over. Any takers?" Aisha kept her eyes on Starlett, pretending she hadn't heard the invitation.

Raven felt one of them should say something, at least to be polite. "Did you see *Scream*?"

Leah threw her hands to her face. "Of *course* not. I would never go to a movie like that. You come out with post-traumatic stress disorder."

Starlett had found some paper to go with her pencil and was busy drawing lines. "No, Star, gimme that," called Aisha.

"It's all right, Oy . . ."

"Oy?" Aisha could feel some serious aggravation coming on.

". . . those are old drafts that are going into the shredder. Who knows, Starlett might be the next Georgia O'Keeffe."

Aisha made a "say what?" face and shrugged her shoulders. "So what y'all be working on in here?"

"Oh, the usual boring paralegal stuff—blue sky filings, document organization, deposition summaries."

Aisha looked at Raven. This time she just pressed her lips together tight. "Oh."

It sounded boring to Raven too but it was still a good job. If you were getting paid and could take care of your family, then why not? Hey, staying at home changing diapers and watching TV wasn't exactly exciting.

"Uh-oh, I think he wants Mommy." Smokey was beginning to fuss and twist in Leah's lap.

"I'll take him. He's tired." Raven pulled a bottle from a baby bag and Smokey leaned toward it.

The office door banged open. Dell was loaded down with a tall stack of binders. Each one had a lot of multicolored tabs sticking out of it. Leah jumped up to help and took a few from the top and Dell dumped the rest on her desk. "Hey, it's Craven Raven and her Band of Bandits. Boy, I didn't know the whole hood was in the office. Brandy only mentioned Raven. I hope you guys haven't been acting too ghetto at my job, especially you, Aisha. This is a blue-blood law firm. Leah, have they been acting ghetto?"

Aisha wobbled her head. "Ghetto? Excuuuuse me, but you so ghetto Jerry Springer invited you to be a guest on . . ."

Raven coughed real loud. Aisha's mouth had already gotten them in enough trouble. And since when did Dell call people "you guys"? She copied everything off Leah. This was a side of her sister she hadn't seen before.

"Your sister and Oy have been great, Dell."

"Oy?!" snickered Dell. "Aisha, did you tell Leah your name is Oy? You are so bad! See, you guys *were* being ghetto. Leah, her name is Ai, like in eye-ball, short for Aisha."

Leah went dark pink. "Omigod, I am so sorry . . . Ai. Don't mind me, the medication will be kicking in any minute now.

85

Moving right along . . . Star here . . . your name *is* Star, right? . . . is on her way to becoming the next Georgia O'Keeffe."

"Is that so? Let me see that picture, Star." Dell examined the page of squiggly lines. "Hmmm . . . not exactly flaming calla lilies but close. So to what do I owe the honor of this visit, Raven? Aisha? Don't even think about asking to borrow any money."

Raven handed her the neatly folded application. "I brought this. Figure I'll try for that college program. Can't hurt."

"Raven, that's excellent! When did you decide? Does Mother know? She's going to be so psyched. I truly thought you weren't going to do it. And you *will* get in. I have to give you a forehead kiss."

Leah smiled. "Awww, that's so sweet. You see, Raven. Dell knows too that you're going to get in."

Raven smiled and for a moment it was as if she was already in the program and on her way to college. "I guess. She was the one who really pushed for the whole thing."

Aisha cocked her head to the side. "And what about me? I'm the one helping her learn them crazy words you can't even say."

"No! *You're* teaching my sister spelling? What *is* this world coming to?"

"It's coming to a theater near you, Miss Paralegal, 'cause I'm subtle, s-u-b-t-l-e, like that."

Raven and Dell stared at Aisha in shock, then everyone cracked up.

Leah noticed the time. "No wonder I'm hungry, it's way past our lunchtime, Dell. I'm sorry, you guys must be starving, walking all that way. Do you eat sushi? It's sooo delicious and totally nonfattening." Aisha blinked in slow motion like she had already fainted and was coming to.

Raven was firm. "Uh-uh, no way."

"Okay. I guess that overwhelming response means no. How about Chinese? There's a great place right across the street. My treat."

Aisha's eyes got big. "You da bomb, Lee!"

Dell was shaking her head. "That is one offer you will live to regret. If you're treating these two, we better go for sushi. It'll cost you a whole lot less."

"It sure will, because I'll be eating only rice," said Raven.

Aisha agreed. "That's word. If it still be alive, I don't be eating it. Y'all saw *Alien* when that giant snake thing, whatever it was, ripped out of that man's stomach and was twisting all wild splashing guts around? That's why I do not be eating any kinda raw meat."

Dell tapped Aisha's shoulder. "Oy. Sushi is fish."

"*You* look like a Oy. Anyway, fish got meat on they bones too. It's still raw and alive. Gimme some beef fried rice or pepper steak well done, and I'm good to go."

"Me too," added Raven.

"Well, then, let's all get good to go," said Leah, "because I am famished. Let's call it an early celebration in anticipation of the spelling bee and Raven's Spell Success victory."

"Word up, Lee," chimed in Aisha. She could already taste her pepper steak and smell Star's beef fried rice.

Dell gave Raven a sideways hug. "That's totally excellent, Raven. Really."

16

Gwen noticed the silence before she was done unlocking the door. No television, no music, no sound at all was coming from her apartment. Raven must've taken the baby out. She stepped inside. Something moved. "Child, you nearly scared me to death! What you doing sitting up here in the quiet? Almost gave me a stroke!" She let her bag drop to the floor and sat down. "You *know* I got pressure. So how was your day?"

Raven placed the cards face down. "Scion, s-c-i-o-n. Seize, s-e-i-z-e. Sieve, s-i-e-v-e."

She felt like she was flying high above all her fears. "And did you know that 'threshold' has one *h* in the middle but 'withhold' has two?"

"Well, I can't say I ever gave it a lot of thought, but now that you mention it . . ."

"That's exactly it. Dell said you have to *think* about words to be able to spell, not just memorize them. Figure out what words go together, have something in common. The only reason people misspell words is because they pronounce them wrong. They spell them the way they say them. For example, spell 'hypnotize.' "

"T-i-r-e-d."

"Come on, Mommy, please, this is important."

"All right, one word. You been carrying on with this stuff for a good long while now. You know I'm with you a hundred percent but your mother's tired when she gets home from work. H-y-p-m-a-t-i-z-e. Now don't bother me no more."

"See, Mommy. You got it wrong because you spelled it the way you say it. You're supposed to say 'hyp-NO-tize.' H-y-p-n-o-t-i-z-e. That's why you have to pay atten—"

"Raven Jefferson!"

"All right, already."

Evening came, bringing the usual noises. Raven paid little attention to the voices singing to the radio, cheering basketball games, calling to one another. For Raven, propped up in bed studying a book full of words, there was the deepest quiet. Not the kind you hear, but a quiet you could feel. Her son lay on his stomach by her side. This had become her nightly practice. With one hand she turned a dictionary page, while the other patted the baby's bottom. The sky grew dark and Raven dozed off.

The spotlight is so bright she squints. Rhythmic foot-stomping booms inside her chest like a bass. The auditorium echoes like a giant stadium. A chorus of voices is yelling strange words. She grips the podium for support, gasping and sweating. A siren shrieks and cherry-red neon letters flash "Begin Begin Begin" on an overhead screen. "Chameleon!" cries someone to her left. She presses her mouth against the microphone. "C-H-A-M-E-L-E-O-N." Pounding applause. Her ears ring. A voice directly in front of her screams, "Eschew!" She can't bring the person into focus even though they're right in front of her. "E-S-C-H-E-W." A chant rises. "Go, Raven! Go, Raven! Go! Go! Go!" "Quinquennium!" "Q-U-I-N-Q-U-E-N-N-I-U-M." "Work, Raven, work!" Words fly at her from all directions, like a hail of bullets. "Tumultuary!" "Succubus!" "Piranha!" "Intaglio!" "Acclimatization!" "Doppelganger!" Raven is amazed to hear herself spell each word perfectly. How can it be? And how come she never noticed her gift before? She begins waving wildly. A joyous smile spreads across her face. The crowd is chanting, stamping, cheering. Some people are just plain screaming.

Raven opens her arms wide, signaling for more. "C'mon, hit me!" she cries into the blazing light. Words swarm her. Xenophobia. Ambidexterity. Oxymoron. A familiar voice bellows. Raven recognizes it, but only barely.

"Feat!"

Whose voice is it? She grabs hold of the mike with one hand, as though she's going to belt out a tune.

The stadium thunders, "RA-VEN! RA-VEN!"

One hand is on her hip. She's a star and it feels great. "F-E-E-T."

The noise settles into a murmur, then fades into utter silence. The neon screen flashes "F-E-A-T."

"I'm sorry, miss. That is incorrect. Thank you for your participation and have a nice day."

That voice. It's the receptionist from National Life Insurance! "No, wait! You can spell it both ways! I mean, I thought you meant feet like, you know, feet that you walk on. Please!"

Raven's chest hurts. There's no air in the place. The auditorium is completely quiet now, almost as though no one is there.

"Miss, I'm sorry. It goes without saying that such an *ordinary* word would not be part of the Spell Success competition. Now please, other contestants are waiting."

"That's not fair, you bitch!"

Suddenly, the floor gives way and Raven drops into darkness, slamming against the jagged walls of a black tunnel plunging deeper and deeper into itself.

Raven awoke with a loud "Unh!" gasping for air. "Damn," she whispered, her chest heaving.

17

The nurse was blunt. "You teens are like jackrabbits with these babies. Not for nothing, but haven't you heard of contraceptives? It's not fair to you or to him," she said, pointing her pen at Aisha's belly. "You're no more than a baby yourself, still living at home, no husband, nothing."

Aisha chewed her bubble gum openmouthed, so it would make that popping noise. She bit at the magenta polish on her thumbnail. Nurse Constantino needed to stay out her business and stop sweatin' her. She'd heard the same speech from the same nurse when she had Starlett. Then it didn't bother her so much. The way she saw it—then—was that so many girls had babies, she wanted one too. So what? Her own daddy wasn't around and her moms ignored her. A baby would give her a mini-family of her own. She'd dress it up real nice, get both ears pierced if it was a girl or one if it was a boy, not be lonely.

Now she knew better. It was lonelier *with* a kid. Your friends without babies stop coming around because you can't go places with them. So you hang out on the benches with the other mothers. But like them, she ended up spending most of her time alone, being somebody's mother. Star was her heart but having still *another* kid . . . Aisha wasn't as happy about it as she had been carrying Star.

Kevin was always rapping about how one day they would all be together. But when? That was just his mouth talking. She wasn't telling Raven just yet. She didn't want no more lectures. Plus, the way Rave was steady tripping these days she'd probably freak out. Always one mood or another with her. Imagine if she *did* end up going to college. It would be all good for Raven but what about *her*? Then she wouldn't have nobody, really. Just two kids.

Nurse Constantino finished writing on Aisha's chart. "Okay, hon, here's your appointment card. Come back and see me in a month. Your next clinic day is the twenty-third. Be good."

"Ah-ight, I will." She read her card. "Aisha Ingram (2 months) has an appointment at the Fort Crest Prenatal Clinic on June 23." Raven's word test would be over by then, thank God. Maybe she'd be back to normal and they could hang without all that spelling madness.

Aisha lifted herself up from the metal chair and walked through the clinic past a row of teens just like her. Because she was big anyway, she was only showing a little, but she could feel the difference. Not sleeping good, being cranky, readier than ever to kick butt. And it felt like her body had big weights tied on it like that swamp thing they had on *The X-Files*. Or was she thinking of that Mafia movie where they roped cement blocks to the stoolie's ankles? . . . She couldn't even remember stuff right anymore.

She stepped off and back on the curb real fast. Everything that rolled was speeding by, bikes, cars, trucks, Rollerblades, everything but a bus. She looked as far down the street as her nearsighted eyes could focus. Nothing. Maybe she'd walk home. The only time Moms would watch Star without complaining was on clinic day, so why not take her sweet ol' time getting back? She liked the feel of the sun on her face. It reminded her of when she used to hang on the beach at Coney Island, hugged up with Kevin. Way before Star was in the picture, when being a teenager was all good. Yeah, it would be a nice walk. But still, they shoulda put the clinic closer to Hillbrook, where all the fly girls live. These oogly-mooglies in Fort Crest didn't need no clinic anyway because no boy would even wanna get them pregnant.

Fort Crest Houses stretched for blocks. Aisha had been walking maybe five minutes when all of a sudden she felt like somebody was watching her. She noticed some girls on a bench, halfway up the block. All heads were turned her way. So, *they* had been clocking her. She kept walking.

Hillbrook girls and Fort Crest girls didn't get along and Aisha was in no mood for nobody's drama. The best thing to do was ignore them if they said something smartass. As she was passing directly in front of the bench she heard a snicker.

"Look what the cat done dragged outta Hillbilly Houses."

"Word up. And it musta been one stroooong cat 'cause she look like two tons of fun."

Two tons of fun. Wait a minute. She felt sweat break out all over her body. *Two tons of fun* . . . Of course! Aisha stopped and looked. The girls with the blond extensions she'd had the run-in with in the elevator were giving each other high fives. And they had three others with them. The whole group had extra-long fingernails painted in different-colored stripes.

"Yeah, that's right, big mama, remember us? You in the Fort now."

The one whose foot Aisha had stepped on stood up. Aisha's heart was beating harder and harder. Her nostrils felt tingly. She knew she could take the two toothpicks by herself, but not the whole squad. Anyway, she had to be careful now because of the baby.

The girl planted herself directly in Aisha's path. "So like what you got to say now . . . *José?*" Her face was so close Aisha could smell her breath. Tootsie Rolls. The other girls crowded around.

"You go, Joyce, we got your back!"

Joyce moved closer. "Huh? Bowwow." She stomped on Aisha's foot. Aisha lunged. The girl fell backward, hitting hard on the ground and Aisha half fell, half sat on her.

"Get her, Joyce! Get her! We got your back!"

Aisha braced herself for the big group attack. Nothing happened. Joyce tried to scratch Aisha in the face but Aisha bit her hand.

The others kept screaming, "Get her!" They watched their homegirl wiggling and grunting. "Goddamn, Joyce gettin' her butt whipped by that elephant-ass Hillbilly!"

"Get this moose offa me!" Joyce cried, pulling at Aisha's ears.

Aisha jammed Joyce in the chest with her elbow, snatched a bunch of braids, and tugged. Someone from behind grasped Aisha by the shoulders.

"What the . . . ? Aisha, is that you?! Get up off that girl before you crush her!" Aisha looked up into hazel eyes.

"Come on before you hurt somebody. Are you crazy?"

Aisha gave a little goodbye kick as Jesse helped her up. Joyce rolled onto her knees and crawled around picking up blond braids.

"Yeah, you *better* run ya hippo ass back to Hillbilly!" Then she sneered at her friends, all eyeing Jesse closely. "Y'all ain't about nothin'! I thought y'all had my back. Don't just stand there like dumb hos. Help me pick up my hair!"

Jesse unlocked the passenger-side door. Aisha climbed in. She was still all fired up and her blouse was torn and soaked with sweat. Her elbow hurt but it was that good hurt you felt when you had just beat somebody down.

"What was up with all that, Aisha!? You know them?"

"Nah, I don't know them scrawny creatures. We had a beef around my way a while ago, that's about it. I dogged her good, right?"

Jesse scratched his head. "Girls brawling. That's too much.

On the ground too, like *WrestleMania*. I thought I was halluci-
nating when I saw you sitting on her."

"That'll show that mutt to mess with girls from the Hill! So,
Jesse, this your Jeep? It's phat!"

"I wish. No, I know this guy from school who lives over
here. He let me drive it around the block but I have to be careful. No license. But I'm driving you home before you get in any
more fights. Seat-belt time."

"Alriiiight! Roll the top down! I want *everybody* to see me up
in here!" The Jeep sped along with Aisha holding her hands up
in the wind, chanting, "Ow! Ow! Ow!"

Hillbrook was only a quarter mile away and they got there
fast. Aisha eased out of the car. Her hip was a little sore.

"Thanks, Jesse. You saved me a token and a beating. I know
her homeys woulda jumped in sooner or later."

"It's cool. Um, how's Raven doing, and the baby?"

"They fine. Smokey's always grinning and slobbering and
Rave's gonna be taking some kind of test to get back in school."

"No kidding! That's great. So she's going back to Ben
Frank?"

"Nope. College."

"College? But she didn't even finish . . ."

"Don't ask me! It's some new thing. You take this big
spelling word test, and if you pass, they send you to college for
free. Something like that."

"I know that program! Spell Success. First you have to do a
really intense summer course. My dad tried to get me in it but

I can't spell to save my life. Wow! Well, tell her I asked about her and that I'm definitely going to call her."

"Yeah, ah-ight. Well, I better get home to my child before my mama go off on me."

Upstairs, Raven's eyes traced the path of a puffy cloud floating high above the projects. All morning she had been in the *q*'s, quarrel: q-u-a-r-r-e-l, quotient: q-u-o-t-i-e-n-t. She needed a break. Resting her elbows on the windowsill she watched some boys dribbling a basketball between their legs. A woman waiting at the bus stop was smoothing her hair down. Raven blinked. Then blinked again. She leaned as far out the window as she could without falling. Was that *Jesse* driving a red Jeep? And was that *Aisha* climbing out of it?!

18

aven couldn't stand the wait. Any other time Aisha would've come straight by. But this was definitely not like any other time. Ai was sneaking around with Jesse! Her best friend and her baby's daddy. She recalled the way Ai had looked at Jesse when they got introduced. It was obvious. She'd been scheming right from the start. That's why she was always asking about them. Raven snatched up Smokey and stormed out. Within seconds she was at Aisha's door.

"She here?"

Mrs. Ingram was in a lumpy housecoat and nappy slippers.

"Hey, Raven. How you doing? Look at that cute little Smokey! Let me give my godchild a kiss."

Raven reluctantly leaned her son toward Mrs. Ingram's pursed lips. And she was *not* Smokey's godmother.

"I'm *still* waiting for the baby picture you promised me. And I don't be asking for every Tom, Dick, and Harry's baby picture, 'cause if it ain't pretty, well . . . Take the girl on the second floor. When she brought her little one home from the hospital it look like one of them scary doll things all y'all kids had last Christmas, the face all squished up like a . . ."

"I'm in a hurry Miss Ingram. Is Ai here?"

"Child, don't pay me no mind. You know me, once I get to runnin' my mouth . . . Yeah, that trifling girl back there in her room, making me wait all morning for her to get her behind home from the clinic, like I don't know how long a checkup suppose to take."

Aisha was laid out on her queen-size bed. "Hey, wassup, y'all? Don't mind my moaning and groaning. Had a rough day, feel broke down, forty years old." No use telling Raven about Jesse so she could get all revved up again for nothing. She best move on. He was all right compared to a lot of them out there, but that didn't mean he was gonna do right.

They watched each other in silence. Raven shifted Smokey to her other hip. It was weird but spelling words were still running through her head. Pummel, p-u-m-m-e-l. Pulverize, p-u-l-v-e-r-i-z-e.

Aisha felt trouble coming. "What's up with you? You can lay Smokey down here next to me," she said, pushing a pile of her clothes onto the floor. Rave seemed extra stressed-out again. Probably them words driving her crazy. The story about the fight would give her a good laugh, cheer her up. "I got something wild to tell you."

"I don't want to hear it, Ai. Spare me your phony confessions."

"Excuuuuse me?"

"Don't play yourself, Aisha, trying to act innocent. I've known you my whole life, you're like family to me . . . and this is what you do . . ."

Ai sat up. "Raven, don't be coming in here talking out your neck. I already had one fight today and I sure as hell don't feel like having another one."

"Oh, so you two fighting already? Good!"

"We two who?"

"You and Jesse, that's who! I saw you get out of his car, Ai, not even ten minutes ago, so don't even try it. We may not be together but he's still Smokey's father and you still are, or at least were, my best friend!" Raven covered her eyes with her hands.

Aisha half wanted to holler out laughing and half wanted to break wild on Raven. But the girl was so pitiful, blubbering and snotting like a baby with a cold . . . She put her arm around her. "Don't you know me better than that? Jesse gave me a ride home from Fort Crest. Matter of fact, he showed up in the middle of a fight I was having with one of them blond wenches we had that static with in the elevator. And you know what, if we wasn't like sisters I would lay you out right now just for *thinking* that way. The only reason I wasn't saying nothin' about it was 'cause you trying to learn all them words for that test and the last thing you need is to get all tripped out again about some boy."

Raven stopped crying. "I don't know . . . when I saw . . . I'm

101

sorry, Ai. Maybe I *am* bugged. You got a tissue? I deserve to get my butt beat. Go ahead. Beat it. I want you to." She pulled away from Aisha and bent over. "Beat my butt, Ai."

This time Aisha *did* bust out laughing. "Get that thing outta my face. I wish that bee would hurry up and *be* over so you can take your butt off to that summer school before you end up in the crazy house. Me and Jesse . . . I can't believe you went there." Aisha's laugh got Smokey to laughing too.

Raven wiped her eyes and blew her nose. She sure was crying a lot lately. After the test she was going to treat herself to a whole day of fun, maybe go to Coney Island with Ai and the kids and eat Nathan's hot dogs and ride the bump cars. Or just do nothing. Her mood was getting better real fast.

"So, tell me about the fight!"

Aisha told the tale, making herself look extra good. "I had that mutt in one of them Hulk Hogan headlocks, banging my fist into her face, right, and then this other skeezer jumped on my back. I twisted around real fast and when she hit the concrete I pinned her down . . ."

"No way!"

"And that's when Jesse drove up."

"It sounds like those girls are lucky he did. So . . ." Raven paused so she would seem more chill, just being casual. "How is he? I thought he lived in one of those Clinton Hill brownstones . . . Why was he way over there? Did he . . . say anything . . . you know, mention Smokey or me?" At the sound of his name, Smokey kicked his legs in the air.

"Chill, Raven! I can't answer fitty million questions at once.

Get a grip. Yeah, he okay, yeah he live in Clinton Hill, and he told me he was hanging with friends in the Fort. I gotta lay back down." No sooner had her head hit the pillow than she said, "That's right! I almost forgot. He said he was gonna call you."

"Why didn't you tell me?!"

"Because . . . he's mines and I love him!"

"Very funny, Hulk." Raven flopped down on the bed. "And what were you doing in cheesy Fort Crusty? Your mother said something about a checkup?"

The chipped plaster on the ceiling got real interesting to Ai all of a sudden. She watched it.

"Hello?! Earth to Ai. What took you to the Fort?"

"I was meaning to tell you this before but I didn't want to hear your mouth. Only my moms know. I was at the clinic."

"The prenatal clinic? Are you . . . ?"

"Two months down, seven to go. Yes, it's Kevin's. And don't start sweatin' me." Raven exhaled like she'd been holding her breath too long.

"And you're out there fighting?"

"That was no big thing. I didn't even work up a sweat."

"What're you going to do now?"

Aisha made like she was thinking. "I'm going to Disney World!"

Raven didn't even smile. "This is serious, Ai. You have one, soon there'll be another one . . . I mean, what's Kevin saying? Anything?"

"What you *think* he saying? 'We gettin' hooked up real soon . . . I gotta get myself together a little more is all.' "

"Have you thought about maybe . . ."

"Hell no. Keepin' it. What's the point? Maybe if I was on my way to college like you or in some fancy job like Dell it might be different. But me, I'm doin' nothin' and going nowhere anyway, so why not have another one?"

"If you think like that, you *will* go nowhere. You can't just stop trying. You got to keep on keepin' on."

"That's a song, Raven. I gots to deal with the real. I ain't smart like you or the pushing-ahead type like you or full of dreams like you. The closest I'm ever gonna get to a college is if you make it in and invite me for a visit. I ain't you. I'm me, Aisha Ingram, food-stamp-collecting single teenage mother of one going on two getting fatter every day. But still lookin' sexy for when the right fly guy step up. And ya *know* that!"

Raven was quiet. Aisha managed a weak smile.

19

The phone message light was blinking red. Raven carefully placed Smokey in his bassinet. How had she not heard the phone ring? She and the baby had been dancing. Maybe the music had been turned up louder than she realized. No one had banged on the wall, so it couldn't have been *that* loud. She pressed "Playback." "Hello? Uh, wassup. Umm, my parents wanted me to invite you . . . and the baby, of course . . . to our place for dinner Saturday, June first, at six. That's *this* Saturday. Call me at home. Later. Oh, this is Jesse."

Raven's excited shriek made Smokey bawl. "Ohhh, Mommy's sorry, did she scare the baby?" she purred, kissing his wet lids and nose and cheeks. "That was your daddy. Remember Papa? Your grandparents want you to show them your new dance. Does the baby want to meet the Huxtables? Yes, he does, he wants to say what up, Grandpa, what up, Grandma." Holding Smokey in one arm, she pulled out her Janet Jackson CD, slid it in the CD player, and turned it up full blast. Then mother and son danced back and forth through the apartment.

She barely heard the door being kicked. "Just a minute!" she yelled, lowering the music and dumping Smokey in the bassinet in one smooth movement. Aisha stood in the doorway with her hands on her hips. Raven was all sweaty and out of breath.

"What the hell . . . you got a disco up in here now? I could hear Miss-Jackson-if-you-nasty all the way down on my floor. I thought you was into peace and quiet." She sat down on the couch. The thick plastic squealed.

"I was. Now I'm into peace and hair grease. You have to hook up my braids for Saturday. I have a dinner date."

"With who? Let me guess . . . Urkel the Nerkel?"

"No, he's holding out for you to be his date at the Nerd Disco. With Jesse!"

"Girl, no you're not! Jesse?"

"Yes, ma'am." She played the message for Aisha. They were in the middle of discussing whether Raven should wear her Venus Williams beads in her hair (too noisy), what she should put on Smokey (his baby shoes, not the high-tops), how she would play it (chill, not excited), and why it was important to go (Raven felt Smokey was part of the Honoré family; Aisha said it was all about the benjamins) when Mrs. Jefferson came home from work.

"Um, hmmm, got caught this time, didn't you? What'd I say about company? Hello, Miss Ingram." Raven could tell she wasn't really mad.

"Hi, Miss Jefferson. I was just helping Rave . . ."

"Ai's giving me advice on how to dress for the Huxtables."

"The Huxta who? That Bill Cosby show? I'm too tired to be figuring out no riddles. Now, what are you talking about?"

Raven replayed the recorded invitation. Gwen was as surprised as the girls, and pleased too, but she didn't let on too much. She worried about all Raven's ups and downs with these people. "Maybe they might turn out to be decent folk after all. But you know as well as I do that your test is right around the corner. It seem to me that the less aggravation you have, the better."

"I know what you're saying, Mommy, but I'll be fine. I won't be going with big hopes or anything, but I really want the baby to be part of his whole family."

"And what about the baby's mother?"

Raven's face warmed. "Whatever happens happens."

Mrs. Jefferson looked long and hard at her daughter and felt like she was seeing herself at the same age, in the same fix. She hoped for the best for her baby girl. "Well then, kids, let's get this show on the road. Look through my closet for something that fits."

20

S on, you are not bringing the streets into this house." That's
what Jesse's father had said when the topic first came up. It
wasn't as if Jesse had asked if they could move in. All he
wanted was to have Raven and Smokey over for dinner. Maybe
if they met . . . His mother, ever the lawyer, was more long-
winded. "Perhaps she is a nice girl, perhaps not. That's not the
issue, Jess. She's one of those housing project girls. That's strike
one. A high school dropout with a new baby and no income.
Strike two. Thus, desperate. Strike three. Jesse, the girl has already struck out in the game of life. She looks at you, at us, and
sees dollar bills . . ."

"Ma! That's so . . ."

"No, let me finish. Do you think you're the only black boy in
Brooklyn with green eyes? You most certainly are not. That
green-eyed baby of hers could be anybody's. I'm sorry but
no, Jesse, your friend is not welcome in our home. Nor her

baby, which is the only fact we really know, isn't it, that it's *her* baby."

Since that conversation, which took place a month ago on the day Jesse met his son, Jesse and his parents had spoken little. Instead, he went to confession daily until the priest finally told him there was nothing to be gained from repeatedly confessing the same sin. He felt like his brain had flipped upside down. He was a kid, not a father, but he couldn't ignore the fact that he had fathered a baby. Jesse knew Smokey was his. He had felt it right away. And he really did like Raven. It just wasn't fair, not the phony way he had rapped to her at that party, not her having to drop out, not his parents' prejudice, none of it. He knew guys his age who'd gotten girls pregnant and not given a damn. They were not his role models. Unlike them, he had a father in his life. Fathers, he believed, were important.

Stevenson High School's guidance counselor was in with the principal. One of the kids, a good boy and a decent student, was showing signs of distress.

"Stephen, I wouldn't come to you if I weren't really concerned. I've talked to his teachers too. They've noticed a change over the past weeks. Late, or no homework, poor class preparation, distraction . . . I've seen it all before and it's not good news. I invited him to come in, shoot the breeze with me. He won't. The girls will come in, cry their eyes out, and get past it, but a boy . . . no way. He'll lock himself up behind a homeboy facade and get eaten alive from the inside out. And I know better than most how often parents are the last to know. The kids keep up a front until sometimes it's too late. If we step in now, we can nip this thing, whatever it is, in the bud. That's why I came to you. Something's troubling your son."

Mr. Honoré turned his fountain pen round and round between his fingers. "I appreciate it, David, I really do. We'll sit down with the boy this evening."

Mrs. and Mr. Honoré talked by phone and agreed to meet at home early to "explore this situation." They knew exactly what was bothering Jesse and wanted to present a united front when they talked with him. Jesse's mother had felt the change right away but had hoped it would pass. In time, he'd forget this girl, go on with his life like other boys, meet a nice young lady from a good family. But nothing was worth Jesse jeopardizing his chances for college, maybe even his health. Jesse's dad was proud that his boy, his young man, really, knew right from wrong and wanted to do right. They both wondered about and dreaded Jesse's intentions, but one thing was clear. It was time to meet Jesse's "friend" and her baby. If only for their son's sake. And if what Jesse said was true, then they had their first grandchild. Yes, they would tell him that evening to extend an invitation to this project girl.

21

Gwen waved the receiver. "Raven! It's your sister!"

Raven listened to Dell go on and on about priorities, once-in-a-lifetime chances—the spelling bee—and bourgeois black folks like the Honorés. First they want nothing to do with project trash, then she's the guest of honor at some fancy dinner?

Raven was nervous too, but God, she was only going to dinner. What could they do to her? Dell made her promise to ask him first, *before* saying yes, why the sudden change of heart.

Jesse had about given up hope when Raven finally returned his call. "I thought you weren't going to call."

Raven had been afraid of what she might hear and had put it off for as long as she could. "Sorry. I was so busy with the baby and studying and all. Well, I guess now you know how that feels. Just kidding!"

"No, you're not. Okay. Touché. So you guys are coming tomorrow, right?"

"Well . . ."

"Well? My folks are really into it and they even went out and got special food. And me too."

"You too what? You bought special food too?"

"No! You're sure full of jokes today. You know what I mean. I'm into it too."

Raven had sworn to Dell she'd ask. But how could she put it in a . . . subtle . . . way? She searched and searched, then just blurted it out. "Honestly, Jesse, I don't get it. One minute, your folks are having cows and calling Smokey a project baby, now it's all 'welcome to my world.' Why'd they change their minds so fast?" There. It was out. She held her breath.

"I shouldn't have told you those things. But they've really come around. One day, out of the blue, they said they'd been thinking about everything, me, you, the baby, and realized they'd been wrong. It was weird. Well, I'd been talking to them all along, you know, explaining things, breaking it down. I suppose it finally sunk in. Parents don't always rule, after all. So you coming?"

Raven said she would.

22

The bus was packed with Saturday shoppers. Through the window Raven saw Jesse waiting at the corner. She adjusted Smokey's cloth cap, picked up the folded stroller, pressed through the crowd, and stepped onto the sidewalk.

"Let me get that," said Jesse, taking the stroller. "The directions were okay? You look nice." So did he. He had done something to his hair and was wearing beige slacks and black shoes instead of his usual baggy jeans and sneakers. Raven had that butterfly feeling in her stomach.

"Oh yeah, no problem. I got a transfer to the Number 31 bus and it came straight here. Your hair's different?"

He rubbed his hand over his new haircut and looked at the ground. "My mom made me . . ." Awkwardly, he tried without success to release the stroller. Raven snapped it open and strapped in Smokey. Jesse knelt down and kissed his son's head. He didn't kiss Raven. She reminded herself not to have any expectations. They walked a block and a half and turned onto a tree-shaded street lined with identical brick three-story houses. "Here we are. You in *my* hut now," he joked.

"Jesse, before we go in I have to tell you something. You're corny."

He laughed real hard. "I know . . . but I try."

The ceiling in the living room was higher than any Raven had ever seen and glass was everywhere. Thick glass sliding doors, candle-shaped glass electric lights, a miniature glass grandfather clock on a large wooden desk with curved feet. There was burgundy carpeting, a black leather sofa with a pair of matching armchairs, and a fireplace, above which hung a painting of a black couple in ballroom clothes. Smokey started crying. Jesse took the baby and held him against his chest, patting him.

The sounds brought Mrs. Honoré from the kitchen. Her dark leather shoes looked real soft. She had on a blue tailored dress and wore her hair in a short natural. Hazel eyes. Raven swallowed. Jesse, holding his son, turned red.

"Mother, this is my friend Raven and . . . her . . . the baby."

"And does the baby have a name, Jess?"

"Oh yeah! Meet Smokey."

"Smokey, is it? How . . . unusual. But such a handsome fellow. What a stylish cap. Come here, little Smokey Bear." Smokey gave her his best gum grin. "That's a good boy . . . Raven, is it? It's a pleasure to meet you, something that should've happened sooner but with our busy schedules . . . Have a seat, dinner's almost ready. Can I get you something to drink, some soda?"

Raven's throat felt tight and dry. "Thank you, Miss Honoré. A grape would be good."

"I'm terribly sorry, Raven, we don't have any fruit at all."

"Umm, I meant grape soda."

Jesse laughed out loud.

"Is that nice, Jess? My son isn't always as gracious as we'd like him to be. I'm sorry, we're a Coca-Cola family. But I'd be happy to send out for something else."

"Oh no, that's okay, Miss Honoré, really! Coke's fine."

"Jess, go get Raven a Coke from the fridge. Stephen, the kids are here!" Jesse trotted off to get refreshments and Raven followed Mrs. Honoré into what she called the "salon."

Smokey snuggled up against Mrs. Honoré's chest. Raven eased down onto the soft leather couch, feeling like she was sinking deeper and deeper. Mr. Honoré appeared, wearing a yellow sports shirt, pants like Jesse's, and brown loafers with yellow socks.

"So this is the little lady we've heard so much about. It's a pleasure." He stuck out his hand. "Stephen Honoré, Jess's dad. I see you've met my wife, Nieda. Jess's sister is staying up at Bryn Mawr for the summer or she'd be here too. Sweetheart, what's the course Ashley's doing?"

"Italian Renaissance painting. Which we're hoping to persuade her to change to pre-law in the fall."

Raven's eyes traveled from one adult to the other. Yawn, yawn, yawn.

"And please," he said, "call me Stephen, or I'll feel old. That's what happens when you're around kids every day and they keep looking younger and younger each year but you don't. Nieda, let the old man greet the new baby." Smokey sure was getting handed around a lot, Raven thought, but he seemed to be liking it.

"Nice to meet you Mr. . . . um, Stephen."

Jesse came in carrying a shiny tray covered with bottles, cans, a baby's bottle, and four thin glasses filled with ice. Mrs. Honoré poured the beverages. Raven wondered why they couldn't just drink out of the can. She was glad to see a bottle of apple juice for Smokey.

"Thank you, Miss Honoré."

"Nieda, please."

"Nieda."

Jesse leaned toward his dad, who was still holding Smokey. "Can I feed him?"

"That's something you'll need to ask the mother."

Raven nodded. Jesse's parents cut glances at each other.

Mr. Honoré lifted his glass. "To new friends."

Raven prayed her glass wouldn't break from being clinked so hard.

"Jess tells us you're in the Spell Success program and will be heading off to college in the fall. And you're holding down a job too? That's very courageous of you, Raven. It's an excellent program. I'm on the Board. Did you know?"

Raven squeezed her glass. Why did Jesse have to mention her tacky job at Catfish Corner? She'd quit that dump ages ago.

"No, I didn't know that . . . Stephen. I signed up for the test. I can't really say what's going to happen but I'm studying a lot."

Mrs. Honoré had a brilliant idea. "My husband knows a number of spelling tutors who help the kids prepare. We had one for Jess, but that's another story. If you need a name . . ."

Did they think she was too project to learn how to spell? "No, thanks. A friend in my building is working with me. We don't need any outside help."

Outside help. Mr. Honoré liked her defiant spirit. Maybe the kid might make it after all. With that competition two short weeks away, she'd *better* have help. "I have no doubt whatsoever, young lady, that you'll succeed. The kids we get from backgrounds like yours are often more motivated and mature, frankly, than the ones who've had an easier time of it. I don't know if Jess told you I'm a school principal. I can see right away, it's in the eyes, who has what it takes and who doesn't. Half the students we get these days, all they want is . . ."

"Dear," interrupted Mrs. Honoré, "let's not bore the kids. They're probably starving. Shall we move to the dining room?"

Raven wanted to say, "Yes, let's not bore everybody into their graves," but she wanted more to make a good impression.

The kitchen was separate from the room where the table was set. The plates and saucers had matching flower designs and there were a lot of different knives and forks and spoons on both sides and even at the top of the plates, all for one person. A high chair with a bib and baby food was placed between Raven and Mrs. Honoré, who held Smokey on her lap.

117

"Doris, who's been with us since Jesse was a baby, cooked a special Haitian meal for today. You can learn a lot about a culture from its food."

"Absolutely," added Mr. Honoré, "history doesn't just come in books, it's also on the table. We have blackened fish, spicy beans and rice, fried plantains and okra. The green salad has a special dressing Doris created herself. *Bon appétit.*"

The family discussed politics, tennis, and colleges. Raven mostly listened. She didn't know much about those topics, but when the conversation turned to music and movies she joined right in. Jesse was right, they *were* old-fashioned. They were against rap, and when Jesse said Missy Elliott was a hip-hop poet his father grimaced and said, "Any relation to T.S.?"— whatever *that* was supposed to mean. Raven made the same face when Mrs. Honoré, who hadn't ever "developed a taste for those Motown groups" and wasn't sure "which one" was Smokey Robinson, said Johnny Mathis was the "be-all and end-all of crooners." Jesse stuck his finger in his open mouth. "I'm gonna barf." Singers didn't get much cornier than Johnny Mathis, but Raven kept that thought to herself.

The new foods Raven tried tasted good but nothing was as good as her mommy's cooking. She was proud that her mother knew how to cook and didn't need a "Doris" to do it for her. The Honorés took turns feeding Smokey, whose stomach was starting to hang over the rubber waist of his little corduroy pants.

By the time they'd finished the crème caramel dessert, Raven was starting to look sleepy and Smokey was already sound asleep. Mrs. Honoré asked her husband to get the car ready. "Our guests are bushed." Raven thanked them for dinner. They said she was "lovely" and wished her luck at the spelling bee. Raven stared as Mr. Honoré pulled a huge Mercedes-Benz into the driveway. Mrs. Honoré kissed Smokey and Raven goodbye. Jesse did too.

The drive home seemed endless to Raven as Jesse's dad droned on and on about the "kind" of kids who "make it" and those who don't. He looked at the boys hovering about the front of Raven's building. They looked hard at his car.

"No, thank you, Mr. Honoré," said Raven when he offered to "accompany" her upstairs. He didn't say it, but she knew why. Shoot, *she'd* have to protect *him*, coming in the projects dressed like Tiger Woods.

Mommy had waited up. "We survived," whispered Raven, Smokey dozing in the stroller.

"Of course you did, baby, the Jeffersons are a surviving people. Here, let me put him to bed and you tell me all about it."

The furniture, the food, the better-than-everybody parents, Raven described it all. "I was kinda jealous in the beginning, because they lived in such a nice place, but I never really felt comfortable there. Everything was too nice, like it was there to look at but not to live in. The couch was pretty but it swallowed you so deep it was hard to stand up. And it didn't have that homey little squeak like ours. But, Mommy, you shoulda seen his mother's face when I told her Smokey's name. Then she said, 'How unusual,' and kept talking about Smokey Bear because she never even heard of the Miracles! And his father was talking like I need a tutor but I turned him flat down. Oh, guess what?! We got dropped off in a Mercedes-Benz. All the drug dealers hanging out on the bench were checking it out, probably jealous that his was bigger than theirs. I have to say, though, they were nice and everything went okay, nothing bad happened. So you and Dell were worried for nothing. See, I *told* you."

Gwen liked seeing Raven happy and excited. "And Jesse?"

"Oh you know, he was the same. Okay, time for bed. Night, Mommy."

23

The scrape of metal on the gymnasium floor hurt Raven's ears. Why couldn't people pick up their chairs? Voices filled the room with a ringing, tinny sound, like a stereo without bass. Dell was whispering inside her head. *Breathe first, Rave, then spell. Take your time with each word. Sound them out, syllable by syllable. Don't pay attention to the other kids.* Raven fondled the pacifier Mommy had slipped in the pocket of her jacket. *No, Mommy, that's so corny.* Gwen insisted it would bring good luck, that a child could give you strength.

A woman in a maroon pinstriped sleeveless dress walked on stage. She must be the emcee. E-m-c-e-e. The podium where she stood had a microphone stuck in it. She asked families, friends, and spellers to please be seated quickly. To the right of the podium was a desk with a fishbowl full of paper. To the left, a table holding a pitcher of water and paper cups.

Family members and guests filled the unreserved rows of

chairs. Raven was in the second row, the one reserved for Spell Success applicants. It was Friday morning and sixteen teens were seated together clutching programs with their names in them. They fixed their blouses and ties and jackets, smoothed down their hair or pushed braids back, and stole peeks inside dictionaries.

The arrow on the "Judges and Pronouncers" sign pointed to the chairs in the front row. Three tables with microphones, pads, pencils, and dictionaries were set up. Jesse's father was sitting with the judges, neat in a business suit, white shirt, and tie. He was acting real official and barely glanced her way.

Raven felt squirmy. The jacket she had on was Dell's and it was too tight. But she couldn't take it off because of the sweat stains she knew were on the armpits and back of her blouse. A thick-haired girl winked at Raven and kissed a balding examiner on the cheek. Dell's office mate, Leah, and her dad. Raven sought out her family, gathered at the rear of the room. Mommy waved and made believe she was clapping her hands together. Dell was feeding Smokey from a bottle. She gave Raven a big smile. Aisha punched the air with her fist. She'd left Starlett at home, she said, so her hands would be free to "throw down" if the judges cheated Raven.

Raven had to go to the bathroom, again, even though she'd just gone. Mr. Honoré sitting all stiff in the first row made her more nervous. Failing in front of her own family was one thing, but people like him expected so much. At least Jesse wasn't there. That would really stress her. His folks wouldn't let him miss school for something about her, that she knew.

The emcee tapped her finger on the microphone. All spellers were kindly requested to place any dictionaries, thesauri, word lists, and other study materials on the floor beneath their seats. Thesauri? T-h-e-s-o-r . . . T-h-e-s-a-w . . . Raven felt panicky. She gazed at the pitcher of water. Leah's father stood, walked onto the stage, and spoke into the microphone. *Generous donations make it possible . . . sixteen courageous youngsters . . . each one already a qualifier for our college prep summer program . . . society's commitment . . . please welcome the Honorable Elizabeth Tamworth-Jones . . .* He moved aside as the Honorable Tamwhatever approached. You could tell she was used to having her picture taken, because the camera flashes didn't make her blink. She was tall, thin, and looked rich. *Thanks to Spell Success . . . won't give my age away by saying how many years ago . . . coming from the projects . . . a rigorous program . . . as your state senator . . . keep on keepin' on . . .* Cheers and loud applause. Raven felt something crawl down her face. She touched her cheek. Sweat. The speaker asked each speller to stand when his or her name was called and said they were all winners already.

Don't pay attention to the other kids. Easy for Dell to say, she wasn't in the spellers row. Raven concentrated on each face, leaning forward in her seat to get a better look. There were mostly girls, twelve to be exact, and four boys. Two Asian girls sitting side by side whispering, an Asian boy, a couple of girls who looked Puerto Rican, a white boy and girl who looked related, and a brown-skinned girl with straight hair. Raven didn't know *what* she was. Everybody else was black.

She was trying to guess who was from the projects when she heard . . . "Raven Jefferson!" It was her turn to stand. Her heart was pounding. As she rose to her feet, it felt like her skirt caught in her crack. She imagined Aisha busting out, saying, "Rave got mail in the box." She ran her hand casually down the back of her skirt. It was okay. She turned around and faced the audience. Dell held Smokey high overhead and Aisha was cupping her mouth and shouting something Raven was glad she couldn't hear. Mommy touched her eyes with what looked like one of her pie cloths. People she didn't know were smiling at her. Raven stuck out her chest. They were all proud of her, she could feel it. And she hadn't even done anything yet.

All at once everybody shut up. The emcee sat down at the desk, reached into the fishbowl, and pulled out a piece of paper. "Maggie Chang." The girl she called squealed, squeezing and shaking the other Asian girl's hand. Step by step like a child learning to walk, she made her way toward the podium. Raven's stomach hurt. It must be awful to be first. Someone in the judge's row coughed, cleared her throat, and said, "Catharsis." The girl said each letter and waited, her small hands clutched in fists.

"That is correct, Miss Chang. You may step down."

Magic words. Clapping came from the left side of the room.

The emcee asked everyone to be so kind as to hold their applause until the end of the competition. Raven thought "catharsis" ended in c-i-s, like "Francis." She felt as if she might throw up. *Breathe. Don't pay attention.* The woman kept pulling names from the fishbowl and placing the slips of paper in order on the desk. One by one the spellers climbed the stairs. Some moved slowly, others took two steps at a time. A boy tripped on the top step but didn't fall. Raven thought she heard Aisha go "Duh!" and get shushed by somebody.

Raven was sure the other spellers must've been as thirsty as she was but no one had touched the water sitting on the table. Her tongue was rough as sandpaper. Kids ran, strolled, and strutted to and from the stage. They beamed or stared or grimaced, depending on what happened once they got up there. Before Raven's name came up six people had already misspelled words and were requested to take seats at the side of the room. Most of them played it off like it wasn't a big deal but one boy cried. Raven felt sorry for him. Some of the words were easy, like "phrase," but he got hit with "empyreal." He'd given it an i-a-l at the end. Bad luck.

"Raven Jefferson."

A voice shouted, "Go!"

A lot of voices said, "Shhhh . . ." *Breathe.* She was on stage pouring water into a paper cup. The room was so quiet that if she didn't know people were there she would have thought she was all by herself.

"Puerile."

"P," she said immediately, then stopped. *Syllable by syllable.*

Pew . . . pue . . . pew . . . She recalled pointing as a little girl at smelly boys and hollering, "P! U!" *Oh God, please . . . not on my first word.*

"P . . . u . . . e . . ." *A vowel sounds long if followed by an* e. . . . "r-i-l-e."

"That is correct, Miss Jefferson. You may step down."

The same voice, which Raven recognized as Aisha's, yelled, "Yesss!" and was answered with "Shhhhhh!" On the way to her seat Raven looked at her mother and made a face. Gwen nodded and clapped the air.

A wheel was whirring inside Raven's chest. Three more boys and a girl were sent off. The examiners announced word after word after word. There was no way to tell if you might get a short tricky one like "quay" or a dumb one like "chugalug" or one of those long ones that sounded hard but was easy if you sounded it out, like "valedictorian." Each time Raven was on stage, she'd stop at the water pitcher. The smooth glass handle gave her something to hold on to. Other spellers began to do the same thing, like maybe they thought it was helping Raven get her words right.

Soon the water was gone. And so were twelve spellers. Only four slips of paper remained on the emcee's desk. Two men, each carrying two chairs, appeared on the stage. The audience clapped. The men bowed. Raven expected the woman to say that thing about holding your applause but instead she smiled. She said the four finalists were requested to take seats on stage. Only girls were left. "You may applaud these impressive young people," she said. "Though only one will win the full college scholarship, they are all headed to college, and that makes them all champions." Shouting and barking and stamping mixed in with applause. People were yelling names. "RAVE PARTAAAAYY!" rang out. Her gaze found Aisha and they both made buck eyes.

"Rosa Walker." Rosa had no problem with "vicar" and held up both fists as she took her seat. Raven had drunk so much water that she had to pee. "Raven Jefferson." She spelled "harangue" and sat down. "Annie Chang." Her sister Maggie cried out from her seat among the other disqualified spellers, "Annie!" The emcee let it go. She probably knew sisters had to stick together. Raven was relieved when Annie spelled "verdure" right. Something about the way she always balled up her hands in a fist just like her sister made you kind of root for her. "Vijaya Ramanatsoa." They gave Vijaya "geoduck." Raven felt bad that she got such a weird word. "Uh, g-o-o-e-y-d-u-c-k." "I'm sorry, Miss Ramanatsoa." The girl's face went white. What kind of trick word was that anyway to ask somebody? If Vijaya was wrong that meant it wasn't spelled anything like how it sounded. That wasn't fair.

Only three spellers were left. Rosa's turn came again. She breezed through "curriculum." Raven easily spelled "pseudonym." When Annie heard the pronouncer say "cochlea," she made a face so funny that people in the audience chuckled.

In a loud voice, the emcee said, "Quiet!" and quiet is what she got.

Annie's mouth was too close to the mike and she sounded

all crackly. "C-o . . . let me think for a sec here . . . c-o-c . . . hmmm . . . okay . . . c-o-c-l-e-a-r?"

She stumbled on her way down the steps and squeezed past spellers' legs to take the seat next to her sister. They hugged for a long time.

All eyes were on the remaining two girls. And their eyes were on each other. *Don't pay attention to the other kids. Breathe.* Rave inhaled a lot of air but that only made her have to pee more. If Rosa went before Raven and messed up, Raven could win—provided that she herself didn't mess up. But suppose she got something like "geoduck" or "cochlea," words she couldn't have spelled either? Then they'd have to keep going until one of them made a mistake and the other didn't. Raven's hand slid into her pocket and she squeezed the pacifier.

"Rosa Walker." Rosa crossed herself like she was in church and kissed her fingers.

"Chasten."

She smiled and brought her face close to the mike. "C-h-a-s-e-n."

A low groan rose in the room.

"Jesus, I *knew* that word," she sighed.

"Raven Jefferson." Raven's knees felt rubbery and she leaned against the podium.

"Quinquennium." Someone gasped.

"That ain't right!" shouted Aisha, jumping to her feet.

"Please!" commanded the emcee. Aisha sat down.

Raven breathed. "Q-U-I-N-Q-U-E-N-N-I-U-M."

A racket exploded in the auditorium. Did I win? She'd won!

128

Flashbulbs and handshakes, flowers and a framed certificate, strangers saying her name, that Honorable Tam-something woman handing her a small white business card with her name and phone number on it, Mr. Honoré congratulating her . . . and there was Mrs. Honoré excitedly talking to Mommy, and Jesse standing right there grinning! Then everybody was on stage, Mommy holding Smokey, laughing and crying at the same time, talking about her pressure and Dell cheering. Aisha had taken over the mike and was chanting, "Hillbrook in the house! Hey! Hillbrook in the house! Hey!" Raven was so happy she forgot she had to pee.

24

That very afternoon Raven took Smokey back to Franklin High School. The stroller attracted so much attention in the halls that Raven felt like she was in a two-person parade. Heads turned and eyes followed her. A few people she knew ran over oohing and aahing.

"Lemme see . . . oh, he's cute."

"How old he is now?"

"Do he take more after you or . . . the father?"

"So you back in school with a baby? Cool."

Raven gave them all a smile and a friendly answer. "Smokey's six months." "I think he looks like both of us." "I definitely am, but not here." It was awkward being in the building as a mother instead of a student, but Raven's spirits were high.

She followed the signs to the administration office and backed in, pulling her baby after her. Miss Jarrett was alone, reading a newspaper. She was thought to be the oldest person in the school, maybe even older than the principal. All Raven knew was that Miss Jarrett was old enough to have blue hair, so she must've been up there.

"Raven Jefferson, my, my . . . How's that sister of yours, still in college? Come over here and let Miss Jarrett give you a hug." The old woman smelled like mothballs. "And I suppose this is your . . ." She looked at Smokey, handsome in a light blue jumper. "I was so shocked when I heard . . . a nice young lady like yourself. But you young girls these days are much faster than when I was growing up, with all this getting pregnant, dropping out of school. Don't get me wrong, though, every child is a blessing and I know he'll be one too. Still, it must be tough on you, especially now with graduation coming up. All the other students off to start jobs, a few even going to college. I feel for you, I do. But listen to me going on and on like an old lady. What brings you and your little fella to school today?"

"I came to get a refund for the cap, gown, and class ring I ordered," explained Raven, pulling a slip of paper from the baby's carry bag. "I have the receipt."

Miss Jarrett raised her chin so she could see better through her half glasses. "Hmmm, yes, fine, this looks like the real thing. You wouldn't believe how many kids come in here with some ol' piece of paper, phony as a wooden nickel . . ."

Raven had prepared herself for this meeting. Miss Jarrett was so annoying, sitting there fumbling around in the cashbox, mumbling, "Such a shame, such a shame." She pulled out a handful of wrinkled singles and fives. "A week before graduation and you're in here getting your money back. With a baby.

131

Your poor mama . . . it's always the mothers who suffer. In today's world the Lord moves in mysterious ways. You want little bills or big bills?"

"Either one's fine." Raven counted the money Miss Jarrett gave her and stuck it in the front pocket of her jeans.

"Will you be coming to the ceremony anyway? It's such a beautiful thing to see our young people all dressed up and . . ."

"I doubt it. I'll be too busy getting ready for college. Bye, Miss Jarrett."

The old woman pulled off her glasses. "But how . . . ?"

"Like you say, the Lord moves in mysterious ways. See ya." Raven and her son left through the main door.

25

The dinner table was covered with a white tablecloth. Matching plates had been brought out for the occasion. Raven was going to college—Gwen had absolutely no doubt about that—as soon as she finished the summer program. Jesse was calling all the time, dropping by. He seemed like a good boy, responsible . . . maybe. The parents, they were a trip, but they loved their grandchild and that was the important thing—family. Yes, indeed, there was no keeping the Jeffersons down. Gwen hummed to music, piling a mound of stuffing on the last plate.

"And this one's for the queen bee of the Spelling Bee," she said, handing Raven her plate.

"Bee. B-e-e," said Raven, opening her eyes wide like she was scared.

"Now tell me, how in God's name did you get that last word right?"

Aisha punched her fist into her hand. "Boyee, when they

slammed you with that kinkykinky whatever I was gonna bust some heads right on the spot."

"I learned it in a nightmare I had about the spelling bee."

Dell took a sip of ginger ale. "That's some word. What's really weird is that I saw it for the first time last week in a lawyer's memo and wondered about it. But I was too lazy to look it up."

"So what it mean, Rave?" asked Aisha. "It must got something to do with Dell's hair if 'kinky' is in it."

"Well, I looked up every word from that nightmare I could remember in case God was trying to send me a message. It means every five years."

"Then I was right, 'cause that's how often Dell do her hair."

Gwen stepped in. "Child, show a *little* mercy on the Lord's day, could you? Do you want some more or is this enough? I know you're eating for two these days."

Aisha peered at the smallish heap of mashed potatoes. "Not to be rude, Miss Jefferson, but I'm a *growing* girl . . ."

"Mother, Ai *always* ate for two. Can we say, 'Booty call'?!"

Aisha gave Dell a sharp nudge. "Yeah, well, that's why your hips so narrow the UN wanted you for one of them hungry people posters."

"Ai, shut your mouth with that mess. We do have company today," said Gwen, glancing at the guest.

Aisha was having too much fun to settle down. "*That's* what you call company? Leah so project, they made her sign up for workfare!" She laughed so much at her own joke that tears filled her eyes. Which made everybody else laugh too.

"Leah, just ignore her. We all know Aisha lost her mind years ago."

"I'm doing exactly that, Mrs. Jefferson, don't worry."

Raven pointed at Aisha, who was still laughing. "All I know is if you wake up my child, it's gonna be booty maul, not booty call."

"Raven!"

"Oops. Sorry, Mommy."

Dell lost it. "That was a good one! Booty maul! Ohhh, my stomach . . ." She was folded over with laughter.

Gwen said, "Now you see, Leah, why their mother got pressure."

For a while, the only sounds at the table were "hmmm"s of pleasure and the clink of forks and knives. Smokey was asleep in the bassinet, his lips still sucking on an invisible bottle. Biscuits were passed around, along with corn on the cob, greens, roast pork, turkey, candied yams, and salad. Leah's plate was the first to empty.

"Can I get you something else, hon?"

"Thank you, but no, Mrs. Jefferson. That was so delicious."

Aisha said, "Girl, you got hongry with an *o* written all over your face. You better stop being polite and get some more food before I kill it." She bumped Raven's knee with her own, smirking.

"Well, all right, Mrs. Jefferson, but not a lot." She handed her plate to Gwen. "I guess I'll have a little more of the greens, a biscuit . . . and a slice of geoduck."

Confused, Gwen froze in mid-motion, holding a spoonful of greens. The table erupted in wild howls. She sucked her teeth. "Leah, I see they're starting to rub off on you . . . We best be getting you on the train back to Manhattan before it's too late."

Raven took a long gulp from her can of grape soda. "It was terrible when they sprang that word on Vijaya. I was like, thank you God, for sparing me. What is it anyway?"

Dell said, "I don't know but it's something nasty, I'm sure. Some kind of nasty duck I bet. Leah, you should know, you're into all those exotic foods."

"As a matter of fact, I've eaten geoduck. It's big on the West Coast. I was out with some friends in Seattle and they ordered it. It's like this totally bizarre-looking giant clam but it has a very pleasant flavor."

Raven said, "I bet Vijaya won't be trying it. Geoduck. That was the worst word out of all of them. Well, at least she made it to the finals."

"That's right," said Leah, "so she gets to go to summer school with all the other finalists. And everyone who makes it through will get some money for college—though probably not enough to support a geoduck habit. But only the winner gets a full four-year scholarship."

"Well, well." Raven grinned. "I'm the special one for once."

Gwen patted Raven on the arm. "Yes, you are, Raven."

"Wait a minute now," interrupted Dell. "Don't I get any credit? I mean, I'm the one who kept pushing her to go for it when she was being all project, like 'I can't spell, get outta my face.' "

"Excuse me y'all but if I do remember right I believe it was me teaching her all them words in the first place AND watching Smokey AND giving her them tesses . . ."

"Tests," said Dell with a smirk.

"T-E-S-T-S," said Raven.

"Them . . . tes-ses," repeated Aisha slowly, staring Dell right in the eye.

Leah burst out laughing. "You two . . . really . . . there should be a comedy bee."

Ai took a chewing break, then went on. "So like if anybody should be getting they props it should be me. Amen. Now pass me a biscuit."

Leah leaned toward Dell and whispered, "Props?"

Dell answered loudly, " 'Props' means 'credit' in *project*."

Raven glanced over at her sleeping son. She didn't want to think too far ahead in the future but she sure felt hopeful right then, for him and for herself. Who knew what would happen with Jesse, if they would ever really be a family. He really was more a boy than a man, still "not ready," maybe he'd never be. But the important thing was that she was going to college! And if that worked out, a real job, an apartment in the City, a different kind of neighborhood for Smokey to grow up in. "It's all good in the hood," she said out loud to herself.

"And ya know that!" answered Aisha as if she'd been in on Raven's reverie. They gave each other a loud high five.

"Who saved room for pie?" asked Gwen.

Aisha rubbed her belly. "*I'm* full but my baby want some dessert."

Gwen went to a cupboard in the hallway and returned holding a cloth-covered pie. "This time I hid it because Raven and Dell don't always know how to act around food. To my future college girl." She carefully placed it in front of Raven.

"Sweet potato pie! Yesss. Thank you." Holding the pie in her arms like a baby, Raven looked around the table. "I'm so glad you all could come by for my Sunday celebration dinner. See ya!" She went running down the hall. Aisha gave chase, slamming into the table and nearly knocking over the salad bowl.

"Mom! That's not right!" Dell said, frowning.

"Raven! Aisha!" called Gwen, shaking her head, chuckling. "Those two . . . I mean it . . . they still as silly as when they were children. Watch them come right back wanting milk. So, Leah, Dell says you're going back to school too?"

Leah had just begun talking about her plans when Raven and Aisha returned.

"Just kidding." Raven smiled. "We only had a teeny taste. Mommy, we got milk?" She wished she could stop time right there on the spot and stay that happy always.